Cursed Souls Guest House

by Geoffrey Sleight

All journeys have secret destinations of which the traveler is unaware.

Martin Buber

CHAPTER 1

IT began with the prospect of a great summertime holiday in beautiful countryside. It descended into the jaws of hell.

"The Yorkshire Dales, that's where we should go," my wife Helen suggested as we sat together on the sofa in our two-bedroom apartment. She was flipping through pages of a country living magazine, and had opened a page showing outstanding views of rolling green pastures, hills and dales in the lush rural setting.

The photos were a welcoming sight compared to the outlook from our home in Birmingham, overlooking an endlessly busy main road at the front and an industrial estate at the back.

We had a week's summer holiday coming, and had been wondering how to spend the time.

"Well, what do you think Andrew?" she asked, as I looked across at the magazine photos.

"Looks good," I replied, distracted from watching a nature programme on the TV about tigers. "Don't think we'll meet too many of them in the Dales," I said, pointing to the shot of a tiger leaping at a terrified wild boar trying desperately to escape.

At that moment I didn't realise we too would soon become the victims of a terrifying powerful force intent on our destruction, with cunning far beyond any tiger.

"Be serious," Helen slapped me on the shoulder. "Stop watching the television and concentrate," she commanded.

1

"I'm trying to arrange our holiday. Now I think we should do it as a hiking tour."

"Not sure about hiking. I want to rest on holiday. We can see places in the car." The idea of walking miles was not particularly appealing to me.

"You've become overweight since you got the office manager's job at Mason's Engineering. You need to lose some." Helen had mentioned my increasing size before. I realised the hiking idea was a bit of a ruse she'd been working on for a while.

It was alright for her as an instructor at the local keep fit centre, where we'd first met a few years ago. I was admittedly a lot shapelier then, enjoying regular exercise. Being office bound in a couple of jobs since had changed my lifestyle.

"Okay, we'll do a hiking holiday," I relented. Helen smiled, acknowledging my defeat.

A fortnight later we set off for Carnswold village in the Yorkshire Dales, complete with new shorts, tops, backpacks and hiking boots, heading towards bed and breakfast accommodation which Helen had booked as the base for our week stay.

The route I drove narrowed into hedgerow lined country lanes as we neared the property that would serve as our temporary home. Breaks in the hedges gave views across miles of pastures. Farmsteads and cottages dotted across the plain rose in and out of valleys to the hazy horizon.

The road descended along winding bends with woodland on each side, and crossed a river bridge as we entered a small hamlet lined with stone cottages. The road continued a little further alongside the river until we arrived at Sunny-side, the name of our cottage accommodation.

It was a name to fit the surroundings perfectly. Warm sunshine lighting the field on the other side of the sparkling river, and woodland at the top of a hill beyond. The world seemed restfully peaceful.

The enchantment didn't last long.

Carrying our suitcases from the car, we opened the gate on to a small paved front garden and rang the doorbell. A middle-aged woman with a droopy face answered.

"Mrs Meadows?" I asked. She nodded.

"I'm Andrew Swanson and this is my wife Helen."

"You're early," she snapped.

I looked at my watch. We'd arrived half-an-hour earlier than the three o'clock time of arrival Helen had given in the booking.

"I don't know if your room's ready yet. Wait a minute." She closed the door and left us standing outside.

"Great start," I remarked to Helen.

"Give it a minute," she replied, forever the mediator. "We've probably caught her in the middle of getting things ready for guests."

That I could forgive, but the woman's rudeness annoyed me. Several minutes later the door opened again.

"Come on in then," Mrs Meadows waved her head for us to enter. She led us down a gloomy narrow hallway, bearing faded floral wallpaper, to a desk where we signed in.

"Number five on the first floor," our host barked, hand-ing over the keys. "Dinner's at seven thirty," the woman turned and walked away, entering a room further down the hall and closing the door.

I was unaware Helen had booked an evening meal for us as well, but some food laid on in the evening after a long hike seemed a good idea.

Our room looked drab, a deeply scratched chest of drawers, the wardrobe with a door that didn't close properly and bedside tables that wobbled. The en-suite sink was stained and the shower cubicle hadn't been cleaned.

"Let's try and make the best of it," Helen detected my discontent.

So making the best of it, we spent time taking a riverbank stroll into Carnswold village a short distance away. I saw a pub and suggested I wouldn't mind a holiday pint of beer. The suggestion was met with disapproval.

"No," said Helen, "on this holiday you can have tea, coffee, water and soft drinks. Maybe a glass of wine with evening meals if you're good. You're going to get some of that weight off."

Once again I conceded, and we settled on coffee in a cafe a little way along the narrow cottage lined high street, passing a small sub-post office and newsagent on the way.

After coffee and sandwiches for our late lunch, we continued the stroll down a footpath leading into a wood and out across a field, enjoying the sunshine and relaxation before returning to the unwelcoming lodging for dinner.

The meal was awful. I had beef casserole, which possibly contained the rubbery meat of a cow three hundred years old, and Helen's vegetarian sausages resembled compacted sawdust. Tasted like it too, Helen remarked, pushing them aside on the plate with her fork to attempt the pulp of remaining mashed potato and cabbage.

We looked across at a couple of dinner guests also staying at Sunnyside. Their grim faces showed signs of agreement.

After so called dinner we decided on an early night to be fit and ready for our trekking. Helen looked beautiful as she undressed, her lovely soft face and long, light brown hair, was a familiar sight to me in our everyday routine at home, but in new surroundings my feelings of desire seemed to be newly sparked into life.

"I'm so glad we met," I told her, undressing and approaching. She looked lovingly into my eyes. We kissed and slowly descended on to the bed.

"Aaagh!" she cried, pushing me away just as her back settled on the mattress.

"What?"

"There's a bloody great lump in the bed." Helen rolled to one side and pulled back the quilt. Sure enough, a bed spring from the innards beneath the sheet rose like a small hill in the centre. It was certainly an effective passion dampener, perhaps left like it by the joyless guest house owner I thought.

We settled instead on trying to get a good night's sleep, which wasn't easy, sinking into sagging mattress on either side of the spring. We'd chosen the Yorkshire Dales for its hills and valleys, but hadn't expected to find them in our bed. I was not going to tolerate this place for much longer.

In the morning breakfast was served to us by a man we hadn't seen until now. I presumed he was Mrs Meadows' husband. His drooping face and similar age certainly matched hers. Without greeting he slapped down our breakfasts on the table, bacon and egg for me and a bowl of muesli for Helen, devoid of any other eating choice.

I complained to him about the room and the bed.

"This isn't the bloody Ritz you know," he growled in return. Then stormed out mumbling curses under his breath.

"He's right there," I said to Helen.

"We'll buy some food out," she tried to placate me. "We'll be hiking most of the time. Let's enjoy the daytimes."

Setting off for our first hike, annoyances with the accommodation soon melted away as we crossed amazing countryside, passing sheep, cows and horses grazing in lush meadows.

We'd been hiking for a couple of hours when the footpath led us off a field into a narrow lane. A few hundred yards further up the slope of the lane, we came alongside a high black wrought iron gate, tall red-brick walls stretching away on each side.

The name 'Longhurst House' was embedded in gold lettering on a grey plate set in the sidewall. Through the gate railings we could see a wide gravel forecourt, and beyond a magnificent L-shaped three-storey house with bay windows, crowned by a lantern roof at the corner and gables on each side. We stopped to admire it.

"That place must be very old," I remarked to Helen.

"Some parts of it date back to the 1650s," a woman's voice seemed for a moment to come from nowhere. "It's been extended and rebuilt over the years."

The voice took the form of an elderly woman who appeared from behind the side wall to greet us with a smile through the gate railings.

"Would you like to take a closer look at the house?" she invited, inquisitive eyes set in a wrinkled, kindly face. We nodded that we would.

Wearing gardening gloves, she lifted the latch in the middle of the gate and opened one side. We entered.

The woman had a green apron over her black dress. She removed the gloves and tucked them into the apron's broad front pocket.

"Just doing a bit of gardening," she said. A grass verge with a colourful flowerbed behind ran along one side of the gravel forecourt. On the other side, a lawn split by a paved path fronted the entrance to the house. The red-brick wall, at least fifteen feet high, surrounded the property.

"My family's lived in this house for three generations," the woman told us with pride. "Come and take a look inside if you wish." She led us along the path towards the front door.

"On a hiking holiday are you?" she obviously guessed from our clothing.

"Attempting to get my husband fit again," Helen joked. The woman smiled.

"Silly me, I'm forgetting my manners. I'm Millicent Hendry," the lady introduced herself as we reached the door. "My friends call me Millie, not that I have so many of them now as most of them have died with the passing years. Feel free to call me Millie."

In return I introduced Helen and myself.

Millie opened the sturdy wooden door and beckoned us inside. The entrance hall looked majestic, painted in deep dark red, with ornate coving and half-length wood panelling along the walls. She opened a door into the lounge displaying framed paintings of scenic Yorkshire Dales pastures, a carved wood surround fireplace and valuable looking Georgian chairs.

Another door opened into the lounge, also featuring a carved wood surround fireplace, a large oriental rug, brown leather sofa and a couple of armchairs. More scenic paintings hung on the walls.

At the end of the hallway a glass panelled door looked over the back garden, another wide gravelled area bordered by beds of shrubs and colourful flowers. A door to the side opened on to the kitchen, which was in complete contrast to the traditional setting we'd seen so far. Inside was a modern cooking range, cupboards and work surfaces.

"Health and Safety laws and all that," Millie said apologetically, noticing our surprise at the difference in style. "I used to do bed and breakfast. The old kitchen, flagstone floor, larder and wood burning stove couldn't meet modern legal standards. So a lot of the original has been replaced or covered over for some years now."

Helen and I shook our heads sympathising at Millie's sad parting with the past.

"Pity you don't do bed and breakfast now," I said, lamenting the fact that such a friendly person and wonderful place was unavailable as an alternative to the dump guest house where we were lodging. As I said it, Helen discreetly tugged my arm as if she wanted me to stop going further down that line.

"Well I get the occasional hikers calling to ask if bed and breakfast is available here," Millie replied. "If I like the look of them, sometimes I'm prepared to put them up for a while. Gives me a bit of company since my husband passed away ten years ago."

"I suppose we'd better be making our way back now," said Helen. "We've more walking to do before we return to our lodging and freshen up for dinner."

It was not exactly a welcoming prospect returning to Sunnyside, and heaven knows what foul food awaited for our evening meal, but Helen was right. As we made our way back to the front door, I told Millie about the terrible place where we were staying. We left the house and began walking along the garden path to the forecourt.

"In no way would I wish to interfere with your plans, but if you like, you're very welcome to come and stay here with me for the rest of your holiday," Millie offered. "I can provide breakfast and evening meals, and I have a lovely bedroom that I think you'd find very comfortable."

For me that seemed like an offer we couldn't refuse. Helen's less than enthusiastic face didn't appear so keen.

"Well, we've paid for the place where we're staying," she said. That was true. Because we'd booked at short notice we had to pay full price up front.

"We'll go back and demand a refund," I insisted, turning to Helen. "The place just isn't up to standard for the money."

"I didn't want to cause an argument," Millie intervened. "It wasn't my intention to interfere with your plans."

"You're not. Please don't apologise," I assured her. "I think Helen's just worried about running costs up." My wife gave me a thunderous look as I spoke.

"I'd enjoy your company, that would be enough compensation for the accommodation," said Millie. "My only charge would be for your food, and I can source that at low cost from a local supplier who I've known for years."

I was sold on the offer. Helen seemed to reluctantly agree.

"We'll stay one more night at our lodging and come over to you tomorrow morning if that's okay?" I asked to Millie.

"Perfectly fine," she agreed.

As we stood talking on the forecourt, a man appeared at the open gate holding two alsatians on leads. The dogs saw us and started barking aggressively.

"Quiet!" Millie ordered, with amazing forceful authority for a woman of her age it seemed to me. The animals immediately obeyed, looking almost guilty for making a noise.

"Those are my precious dogs, Rufus and Petra," Millie announced.

The man holding them on the leashes closed the gate behind him and released the animals. They ran to Millie and she bent down to stroke them The dogs looked thrilled to be in the company of their mistress.

Helen grabbed my arm. She was nervous of strange dogs, and large ones like alsatians in particular. A dog had attacked her when she was a girl she'd told me. It left an indelible fear in her psyche. I put my arm round her shoulders to reassure her all was well. Millie noticed Helen's reaction.

"It's okay. They won't hurt you," she added to my reassurance. "They are very obedient, and they know any guests of mine are my friends to be treated with the utmost respect."

As the dogs wandered off towards the back garden, the man who'd brought them here drew near.

"This is my grandson Nicholas, or Nick as we call him," Millie introduced the newcomer. The man was huge. Tall, muscular and wide, wearing a light blue short-sleeved shirt, and navy trousers.

He nodded to our presence saying nothing, just studying us through curious wide eyes set in a large square face, topped by black curly hair.

"Nick takes the alsatians for a walk now and then," Millie continued telling us about her grandson. "And to dog training sessions every Saturday morning in the village, don't you Nick?" she prompted. The man nodded again. It appeared he was not a great talker.

"There's some homemade blackberry and apple crumble in the kitchen I've made for you," she told him. The news brought a smile to the man's face. He left, heading into the house.

"Forgive Nick, he doesn't say much, but has a heart of gold," Millie explained. "His mother, my daughter, and her husband died in a tragic car crash when he was a boy. I don't think he's ever truly got over the trauma. I brought him up and now he leads a fairly independent life working for a local builder. He has a flat in Oxton village a couple of miles away."

Helen and I weren't quite sure how to respond. It was such a sad tale. Millie saw our awkwardness.

"You're on holiday. Don't let me weigh you down with long past family woes," she brightened up with a smile. "Shall I see you tomorrow?"

"Definitely," I replied. Helen gave a half-hearted nod.

"I think you'll have a truly memorable time here," said Millie, as we walked towards the gate to leave. In the event, she was truly right.

Making our way back across the pastures to Sunnyside, I asked Helen why she'd tugged my arm when Millie suggested we could stay at her house.

"I don't know," she replied, "just this feeling about the place came over me."

"But Millie's a lovely lady," I said. "It looks a fantastic place compared to the rat hole we're staying in. Good deal on the cost too."

"I know, I know," Helen agreed. "Just a feeling I have, that's all."

CHAPTER 2

AS expected, our evening meal at Sunnyside descended to the same low level as the previous night. My steak and kidney pie's crust resembled the cracked surface of a dry river bed, with blackened meat chunks on the inside covered in axle grease gravy.

Helen's cod steak was so dehydrated it actually gave a clunking sound when she tapped it with the back of her fork. That made us laugh, but more in irony than amusement.

When I pointed out the flaws in the food to the man I presumed was Mrs Meadows' miserable husband, he told us that's all there was and walked off muttering 'don't know why they bothered to come here'. Once again I found myself in agreement with him.

We suffered another night's sleep resting with the bed spring hill between us, and got up early with the intention of checking out and buying breakfast at the cafe in the village.

When I told Mrs Meadows we were leaving and asked for a refund of the money we'd paid in advance, her normal grim expression deepened further.

"No refunds!" she snarled.

"What's the matter?" the sullen man appeared from a doorway in the hall.

"They want a refund," Mrs Meadows called to him.

"No refunds," he repeated the stonewall reply.

The man began to approach me.

"If you don't like it you can piss off," he shouted.

I began to round on him, so angry I wanted to punch him hard. Helen grabbed my arm.

"Leave it. I booked on the credit card. We'll take it to dispute." Helen's wisdom prevailed. Having a fight would only make it worse, and these idiots were not going to spoil our holiday. We collected our belongings and left.

It was a twenty minute drive to Millie's place. She'd left the wrought iron gate wide open and we parked at the side of the gravel forecourt. As we took our belongings from the car boot, Millie came out of the house to greet us.

"You've certainly brought the fine weather with you," she commented. The sun in a clear blue sky gave a magnificent glow to the property and surrounding hills and pastures.

We followed Millie into the house and up the stairway to the second floor landing. Our room faced the stairs, while further along the landing to our left and right were two other rooms.

Inside was amazing compared to where we'd stayed, furnished with expensive looking period furniture, a four-poster bed with cream drapes, a large en-suite, and gold curtains with looped tie-backs aside the window, overlooking the most beautiful countryside view.

"Wow," I uttered, as we took it all in. "Now we can really enjoy our holiday." Helen was equally impressed.

The first day we spent time taking a short walk over some field footpaths, returning mid-afternoon to rest for a while and make up for the uncomfortable nights we'd spent at Sunnyside.

Millie had asked what type of food we liked, and in the evening she served me a juicy steak with chips, peas, mushrooms and tomato. For my vegetarian wife, succulent salmon with perfectly cooked vegetables, all followed by chocolate brownie with ice cream or custard. Sheer heaven, served in the wood panelled dining room, with portraits of deer and horses on the walls. Sets of unlaid tables around us indicated earlier times when Millie had served more guests in her accommodation.

The comfortable bed in our room also exceeded expectations, and for the first time on this break we were able to enjoy intimacy that had been obstructed at that awful place we'd escaped.

After a wonderful breakfast in the morning, Millie prepared us a packed lunch and suggested we visit Bolton Castle only a few miles away.

"Mary Queen of Scots once stayed there on the run from losing a battle in Scotland. 1500s I think," she told us.

We decided to make that our main aim of the day.

As we hiked along the field footpaths, we heard a panting sound coming from behind. Looking back, two alsatians were rapidly nearing. Helen grabbed my arm in fear. I too was nervous about being attacked, but tried not to show it.

The dogs stopped, beginning to circle us and drawing closer as if wanting to be stroked. I obliged and then realised they were Millie's dogs, Rufus and Petra.

"It's okay, they're Millie's," I reassured Helen. She cautiously approached, and seeing they wanted to be friendly, relaxed and began stroking them as well. They followed us to the castle, which given its long years of history, was still very well intact.

We toured the ancient rooms inside, and coming out again were met again by the two alsatians waiting patiently for us.

Making a round route through different fields back to Millie's, the dogs started to follow us again. Helen and I began to get the distinct feeling the dogs were tracking our movement. No distinct signs beyond them being present. Just feelings.

That evening, Millie served us with more delicious food, and she smiled modestly when I praised her culinary skills.

"I've had plenty of practise over the years," she replied, "cooking for many guests in the past."

I mentioned that her two dogs had joined us on our hike that day.

"They're very friendly, and love romping in the countryside," she said. "You're honoured they like you so much." Millie began clearing away our empty dessert bowls.

Much as we liked the animals, I hoped they weren't going to make a habit of following us. The holiday was a rare moment for Helen and me to share some 'just us' breakaway time together, without feeling responsible for anything else but ourselves.

"We were thinking of walking to Alcott tomorrow, the town about six miles away from here," I told Millie, as she prepared to leave the dining room carrying the bowls. "We drove through it on the way here, and Helen wants to look in a few shops there."

"Oh really," Millie replied, not venturing any further comment. I don't know why, but I thought her tone sounded slightly disapproving of the idea.

We returned to our room preparing for an early night so we'd be refreshed on our excursion tomorrow. Helen remembered she'd left a bottle of hair shampoo in the boot of the car she wanted for her morning shower, and went to collect it. I carried on getting ready for bed. When she came back her face was puzzled and pale.

"What's the matter?" I was concerned.

"There are no other guests staying here, are there?" she asked.

"Not as far as I know," I said, certain that Millie had told us she no longer did bed and breakfast except on rare occasions.

"It's just that I saw a young man in T-shirt and shorts when I reached the top of the stairs. He was standing outside that room door left along the landing," said Helen.

"Well maybe Millie's taken in some other hikers," I suggested.

"That's what I thought for a moment," Helen remained puzzled. "I said 'hello', but the man just stared at me then turned to the door and evaporated through it."

"What? You must have imagined it."

"No, I didn't imagine it!" Helen insisted. "I'm not mad."

""Alright, alright," I raised my hands in a calming gesture. "I'm not saying you're mad."

"I'm really beginning to wonder about this place," Helen's face looked drawn. "I've got a feeling about it."

I put my arms around her.

"Look, I'll ask Millie in the morning if she has any other guests in the house," I promised. "Best now though that we try to get some rest."

"Only ghosts disappear through doors," Helen remained troubled.

"Don't be silly, ghosts don't exist," I assured her.

"Don't bloody patronise me, I know what I saw," she snarled.

"I'm not trying to patronise you. Just trying to keep it all settled. Come to bed. We'll talk about it tomorrow," I kissed her brow.

After a few moments Helen nodded, agreeing to my suggestion. A second night of passion, however, was not on the cards. Helen continually turned restlessly in bed. It wasn't a great night's sleep for either of us.

At breakfast I asked Millie if she had any other guests staying.

"No," she replied, looking surprised.

"It's just that Helen thinks she saw a young man standing outside the landing room door on our left last night," I explained.

"You're the only ones staying here," said Millie. She placed a pot of coffee on our table and left without another word.

"I didn't *think* I saw someone outside the room," Helen snapped at me, "I bloody well *did* see someone."

For the sake of peace I said nothing further to dispute my wife's claim. She wasn't prone to imaginings, though I wondered if this was one.

We set off on our trek following field footpaths to the town of Alcott, blessed with another cloudless, sunny day. Nearing our destination only a mile away, we heard the sound of panting approaching from behind again. We turned. The alsatians, Rufus and Petra, came bounding up to us. I stooped to stroke them and they brushed my legs eager for the greeting. Even Helen bent to stroke them, confident now they meant no harm.

The dogs followed as we continued, reaching the top of a hill and seeing the cluster of Alcott houses and shops not far away in the valley below.

We began the descent. The dogs ran ahead then stopped. As we approached, they started growling at us. Helen remained still as I continued towards them. They began barking, baring their sharp teeth as if daring me to come any closer at my peril. I stopped. The dogs seemed to calm down.

I started approaching them again, reaching out to give a friendly stroke. One of them shot forward, baring teeth again to snap at my hand. Quickly I pulled back.

"I think they're telling us to go no further," I called to Helen, who stood a good distance behind me.

"That's ridiculous," she said, "we can't be intimidated by Millie's dogs."

I agreed and began to walk on ignoring them. Once again they rounded on me barking and snarling.

"Let's stop and eat our packed lunches," I said. "Maybe they'll get tired of hanging around and leave soon."

We sat on the grass, delving into our rucksacks and taking out the sandwiches Millie had prepared. The dogs laid themselves across the footpath a short distance away. After twenty minutes, when we'd finished eating and downed our soft drinks, the dogs were still resting on the footpath.

"They're bloody well shepherding us aren't they," said Helen.

"No, don't be ridiculous," I replied. "I'm sure we can make our way now." I got up and began approaching the animals. They sprang up and started snarling again.

"Told you," called Helen, "they really don't want us to go any further."

"Right, let's see if we can find another footpath to the town," I was determined not to be prevented from going on. Helen stood up, shaking her head.

"I said I had a feeling about staying at Millie's. An omen if you like. I think we should leave the place as soon as possible."

"Now you really are being ridiculous," I dismissed Helen's warning. "I'll tell Millie what's happened when we get back and ask her to stop them following us." My decision did not reassure Helen.

Taking a map from my rucksack, I saw there was another footpath leading to Alcott a short distance away across the field to our right. We diverted walking alongside a hedgerow bordering a crop of ripening corn. The alsatians continued resting, no longer interested in stopping us it seemed.

The new route led to a style crossing a hedgerow into the next field. As we climbed over, that familiar panting sound broke into our sense of freedom. The dogs had taken another route across the field, racing towards us, running in front and beginning to bark and snarl to prevent us travelling any further.

"That's it," I announced. "We're going back and I'll tell Millie in no uncertain terms to stop her dogs following us."

Helen shook her head again.

"We need to leave the place. I'd rather forget the holiday and go home. At least we can get some peace there."

"No, we will not be prevented from getting a decent break," now I was angry, "even if we have to find somewhere else to stay."

Helen was my faithful friend, and I knew she would always do her best to keep me happy. I think it was only for that reason she didn't put her foot down and demand we leave Millie's immediately. But I also realised she was not far from that point, and I'd have to find a way to fix the problem pretty quickly. How I later wished I'd listened to her advice to leave the place straightaway.

******

WE arrived back at the house a lot earlier than planned for the day. The alsatians had disappeared somewhere into the countryside apparently content we were returning. Inside I looked for Millie, but she wasn't around. We appeared to be alone.

Leaving the backpacks in our room we decided to stroll for a while in the extensive back garden, and made our way down the hallway to the rear door opening onto the setting. Beyond the gravelled rectangle stood a line of trees with a paved pathway between them that we hadn't noticed before. Overhanging leaves on the lower branches almost obscured it from view.

Curiosity aroused, we strolled towards the path and ducked under the leaves for several feet before it opened on to a large lawn. Tall shrubs surrounded the edges, which were only eclipsed in height by continuation of the high wall that surrounded the grounds of the house.

At the far end of the lawn stood a wooden chalet with steps leading on to a veranda. We approached and could see the wood was very weathered, but still in good condition. The structure was delightful, reminding us of a Swiss chalet we once stayed in on a skiing holiday.

We mounted the few steps on to the veranda and tried to see through the windows on each side of the front door, but the curtains inside were drawn closed. I tried the front door handle. It was locked.

After studying the chalet a little longer, we descended the veranda steps to return to the house. We were only a few yards away when we heard a key turning in the door lock. It opened and Millie emerged, locking the door behind her.

"Hello," she greeted, catching sight of us. "Have you had a good day?" She came down the steps and joined us.

My fury at her alsatians preventing us getting to our destination had subsided, but I still wanted to make my point.

"You're dogs followed us again, only this time they became aggressive and stopped us going any further as we got near Alcott."

"Did they?" Millie seemed surprised. "I shall make sure they don't bother you again," she assured us. "They're very well trained."

They might be well trained, I thought, but not very well behaved. Certainly not to me and Helen. I held back from voicing the thought, since Millie had given the assurance it wouldn't happen again.

"That's a lovely chalet," said Helen, changing the subject.

"It is, isn't it," Millie agreed.

"We once stayed in one in Switzerland," Helen sounded unusually friendly, which seemed strange after she'd expressed disquiet about the place and our host.

"Could I take a look inside?"

A barrier descended on Millie's face.

"Oh, I just use it for storage these days," she replied. "It's very untidy inside, nothing to see really. I used to rent the chalet to holidaymakers, but catering for lots of people both here and in the house eventually became too much."

It was obvious Millie wasn't going to show us inside the property, and we began strolling back to the main building together.

"You have some beautiful furniture in the house," Helen continued being chatty.

"Yes, much of it Regency," said Millie. "That was my late husband's doing. He was a very successful businessman. Spent a lot time away, often abroad," she continued.

"He paid for the furnishings. Loved elegance. Insisted that if I wanted to run a bed and breakfast guesthouse in his long absences, the place should have the finest furniture. Kind, thoughtful man," Millie looked wistful.

"He loved the old-fashioned world, buildings and art-works. I have some valuable paintings he bought hidden away for fear they might get stolen."

We ducked beneath the tree leaves overhanging the path back to the gravelled back garden.

"My husband's father, Oscar, helped me to run the guest-house business in his retirement, God rest his soul," Millie continued in full flow. "Now he was an immensely skilled man in the art of ....". Her next word was drowned out by loud barking as the alsatians, Rufus and Petra, came racing towards us. "He taught me that skill over a number of years," Millie raised her voice over the sound.

Whatever skill she'd been taught by her father-in-law re-mained a mystery to us, obscured by the dogs noisy excite-ment at seeing their mistress.

"You naughty dogs," she reprimanded the animals, stooping to stroke them. "You mustn't upset our guests. You must let them enjoy their holiday."

I wasn't sure if the telling off made any sense to them. They certainly didn't appear sorry, continuing to happily jostle around Millie as we made our way back inside the house.

Back in our room Helen voiced her unease about Millie, while undressing to take a shower.

"That woman is hiding something in the chalet. She looked very furtive as she was coming out of the place."

"Millie said her husband had bought some valuable paintings. Maybe she keeps them under lock and key in there," I offered an explanation.

"Maybe. I'm not so sure," Helen replied cynically.

"You were very chatty to her in the garden for someone suspicious about her," I said.

"I was trying to pump her for information, that's all. Seeing if she might let something slip."

"The regular detective," I commented. My comment wasn't appreciated. She screwed her face at me and walked off to the shower cubicle.

After dinner we sat with glasses of wine at a terrace table in the back garden. A soft, warm breeze in the evening sunshine made me feel all was right with the world. Not so Helen.

"Let's take a look at that chalet again," she said.

"Why?" I couldn't see the point. The place was locked.

"I don't know why. I won't know why until I discover why," she replied tersely. Reluctantly I agreed to go with her.

Making our way across the gravel and under the leaves overhanging the path, we re-emerged to see the chalet across the lawn. A young man and woman were standing on the veranda outside the front door. It threw us for a moment since the place was no longer being let.

We approached, wondering if Millie had taken in some new holidaymakers who were now looking round the grounds.

"You left your drinks on the table," Millie's voice came from behind. We turned, surprised at seeing her as she held out our glasses of wine.

"Have you got new lodgers?" I asked, taking my glass.

"No," she replied, a puzzled look on her face.

"It's just that there are two people on the chalet veranda," I turned back to point them out. The veranda was empty. Helen saw they'd disappeared too.

"You're the only new guests I've taken in for a while now," Millie answered.

"But there were two people, a young couple, standing on the veranda," Helen insisted.

"If there had been any intruders, my alsatians would have sniffed them out," Millie was adamant. "The lower level of the sun shining through the tree branches at this time of year can cast some odd shadows," she offered an explanation for what we'd seen.

"Now you both enjoy the rest of your evening," Millie smiled, then made her way back towards the house.

"You saw them, didn't you?" Helen rounded on me.

"Yes, well it looked like two people were standing there, but they can't just disappear into thin air." The notion seemed illogical.

"They bloody well can if they're ghosts," Helen protested, angry at my refusal to admit the possibility. At that moment I couldn't accept the possibility that an after-life spirit world existed. But I couldn't offer any rational explanation for what I'd seen either. And neither did shadows cast by sunlight through tree branches, as Millie had suggested, seem a good explanation.

26

"I want to leave this place right now. That woman Millie scares me. The way she crept up on us," Helen was becoming distressed. "Let's settle the bill and go."

"It could take ages to find somewhere else to stay at this time of day," I reasoned. "We just can't let irrational fears run away with us."

Helen calmed down a little, but remained troubled.

"Give it another day. Millie assures us the dogs will be no problem tomorrow. A pleasant hike will make everything seem different, I'm sure." I took Helen in my arms. "Just give it a try. If you're still unhappy, we'll leave straightaway."

We made our way back to the house and up the stairs to our room. As we reached the landing Helen grabbed my arm.

"I'd like to know what's in that room," she pointed to the door on the left where she said she'd seen a young man disappear through it. I couldn't see the point of looking, but walked across to the door and tried the handle. It was locked, as I thought it would be.

"I've seen a set of keys on a hook in that recess under the stairs. Maybe one of them would fit the door lock," said Helen as she joined me.

"I don't think Millie would appreciate us nosing around her house," I replied. "And I can't see the point to it."

"Well I can, and if you don't want to get them I will," Helen turned to walk away.

"Alright, wait here. I'll get them," I snapped. "But quiet, we don't want to alert Millie."

I crept as quietly as I could down the stairway, which wasn't helped by a creaking step halfway down. At the bottom I waited for a moment, listening for any sound of Millie moving around. All was silent.

The keys jangled noisily for a second as I removed them from the hook. Again I stopped to listen for a moment. Confident the coast was clear I rejoined Helen on the landing. I tried several keys in the lock before finding one that turned to open the door. I flicked on the light switch.

Dust sheets covered shapes of furniture and a bed. The sheets themselves were covered in dust. Old cobwebs spread around the walls were also dust coated.

"No-one's stayed in here for years," Helen whispered.

"Well Millie said she doesn't do bed and breakfast anymore, except for some she takes a liking to," I whispered back.

"That's what worries me," Helen replied.

"Why should that worry you?" I didn't understand my wife's logic.

"I don't know. Just a feeling. It doesn't feel right."

At Helen's insistence I found the key that unlocked the room door on the other side of the landing. A similar scene of dust sheets and cobwebs on the walls met us. I closed and locked the door. We turned to go back to our room and saw Millie standing at the top of the stairs staring at us.

"The two rooms are a bit dusty now," she said, sounding as though it was perfectly acceptable for us to have taken her keys and uninvited looked into the rooms.

"Sorry," I blurted, feeling awkwardly embarrassed.

"Oh don't worry," she replied, unphased by the intrusion. "As my guests, I'm quite happy for you to have the run of the house. I'd love you to stay here and enjoy the place forever."

Her perfectly reasonable attitude made me and Helen feel uncomfortable. Surely a normal reaction to people spying into closed areas of your home would invoke anger, upset, surprise. And the way she said she'd love us to stay at the place forever sent a strange chill through me.

"If you give me the keys, I'll put them back on the hook downstairs." As she spoke I detected a scheming grin in her eyes. I handed the set to her.

"Thank you," she took hold of them. "Well I expect you'll want to get some rest now. Any plans for tomorrow?"

"We're thinking we'll make our way to Alcott town again. Helen wants to look in some shops there," my words came falteringly, still feeling back footed at being caught spying on her property.

"The weather forecast is good," Millie smiled, "and I'm sure my alsatians will give you no trouble." She descended the stairs, leaving me still steeped in embarrassment as we returned to our room.

"I knew we shouldn't have looked in there." My feeling of being a fool turned to anger at Helen making me do it.

"Wasn't that creepy, Millie suddenly appearing like that?" Helen ignored my annoyance.

"I suppose you think she's a ghost too?" Now I was doubly annoyed.

"Don't be silly. I get the feeling it's her doing the spying, and she gets the dogs to do it for her when we're out."

"What, they give her a full written report?" I rubbished her suggestion while undressing for bed. "You really are flying into the realms of fantasy. How do you get these ideas?"

"I don't know. Just a feeling."

"For God's sake, stop saying that," my annoyance at being caught out by Millie still made me feel sore.

"Stop being so bloody precious," now Helen sounded angry. "I think that woman is dangerous. Don't ask me why. Yes, it was a bit embarrassing, but it happened. We move on."

"What d'ye mean dangerous?" I sat down on the bed removing my trousers, and stopped to look at Helen for an explanation.

"I think she's a bit loony."

"What?"

"I don't know, just a...."

"....feeling," I finished her sentence. Shaking my head wearily, I carried on undressing. "Let's get some rest. I've really had enough for one day."

CHAPTER 3

NEXT morning at breakfast, Millie's manner was bright and cheerful as if the event of the previous night had never taken place. That made me feel even more diminished, as if the saint had forgiven the sinner.

"Another sunny day for your hike," she said, placing a pot of coffee on our table. I smiled at her sheepishly.

"She puts on a fantastic act," Helen whispered, as Millie returned to the kitchen.

"Let's just forget last night," I replied, wishing the event had never happened.

We finished breakfast and once again set off for Alcott, enjoying the amazing sunlit meadows and hills free from the alsatians following us. When we reached the same spot where yesterday the dogs had stopped us going any further, we looked back to make sure they weren't on our trail. They weren't. We descended the hill into the town.

Over the next few hours we visited the local museum, wandered around shops, and chilled out enjoying coffee and cake at a cafe in the market square, where stallholders plied their goods to the bustling shoppers. At last, we were beginning to relax.

On the way back to our lodging we decided that even though we hadn't been troubled by the dogs, it was probably time to move on from Longhurst House.

Helen's apparent sighting of a ghost outside the room on the landing, and the couple we'd seen on the chalet veranda suddenly disappearing did seem odd. I had to agree, something didn't sit easy about the place. Definitely time to move on. I'd tell Millie we had plans to explore a different part of the region.

As we neared the property, my phone started ringing. It was my sister, Julia. She knew we were on holiday in the Yorkshire Dales.

"No, Sunnyside where we were staying in Carnswold was rubbish," I told her when she asked how everything was going. "We relocated to a place a few miles away. A grand old house with a tall wrought iron gate and high wall surround. But we're..."

The phone beeped and cut out. I tried calling back, but the signal remained down.

"My sister, Julia," I told Helen, replacing the phone in my backpack. "The signal cut off."

"I gathered that," she replied as we reached the gate and lifted the latch to enter the grounds of the house.

"Well we had a good day without the alsatians bothering us, maybe we'll stay here just another night and move on tomorrow after breakfast," I suggested to Helen when we'd returned to our room. "It's getting a bit late in the day to start finding new accommodation."

Helen wasn't overly enthusiastic about the idea, but agreed it would probably better to look elsewhere when we had a full day ahead.

"But we leave first thing tomorrow," she insisted.

At dinner I told Millie we'd succeeded making our journey to Alcott without the dogs stopping us.

"I'm so glad," she said, placing our meals on the table. "I gave them strict instructions to leave you alone."

Later, when she was serving the desserts, I told her we'd be leaving after breakfast in the morning.

"I hope my dogs haven't put you off staying," she appeared crestfallen.

"No, no," I lied, "we just want to tour a wider area." Millie seemed to accept the answer.

A short time later as we were drinking coffee she returned to the dining room.

"I'm so sorry," she began," but a plumbing leak has soaked the carpet in your room. I've taken the liberty to move your belongings into another room."

"Has it damaged any of our things?" Helen sounded alarmed.

"No, it's just that the carpet's soaking wet," Millie explained. "I've cut off the water supply to the room, but I can't get a plumber out until tomorrow. And then it'll take days for the carpet to dry."

"Well it's just for one more night, so I'm sure another room will be fine," I said.

"It's not well furnished like the one you've been in," Millie apologised, "but it should be okay for the night. I just need to make up the bed and put in some toiletries, so I've left glasses and a bottle of wine for you on the back garden terrace table while I do it."

Helen and I sat in the evening sunshine for about an hour, drinking the wine and chatting about our next destination in the Dales, when Millie came to take us to our new room.

She led us down a side corridor leading to a flight of winding wooden steps opening to a landing at the top. This part of the house was unfamiliar to us. I'd noted the side corridor before, but thought it was an out of bounds private area leading to Millie's accommodation. She opened a door on the right side of the landing and showed us in.

The new room was no picture. The patterned wallpaper faded, the wardrobe and dresser deeply scored with some handles missing, and the en-suite had black mould invading the shower grouting. There was no window, but at least the double bed looked freshly made with clean quilt and sheets. Millie had also hung our clothes in the wardrobe.

"Sorry about this," Millie apologised again," but as I said when you arrived, I'm not charging you for accommodation." She took the keys from me for the old room and gave me a set for the new, then left.

Helen checked to make sure our backpacks and other possessions had been transferred too.

"My phone's missing," she announced, after making a thorough search.

"You're always losing your phone," I replied a bit pompously, knowing it was not unusual for her to mislay her phone.

"It's bloody well missing," she exploded at me. "Have you got yours?"

I looked in the pocket of my backpack. The phone wasn't there. I searched through the rest of it, then the pockets of a couple of coats, even in the dresser drawers where we hadn't put anything yet.

"My phone's missing too," I admitted, my pomposity deflated.

"She's taken them," Helen's face reddened with fury.

"I'll go and find Millie and ask her if she's seen them," I said.

"Ask her what she's done with them more like," Helen demanded. "In fact I'll do it."

"No, I'll do it," I attempted to calm her down. "Just relax. I'll be back in a minute. Millie might have left them in the other room."

"Well you can't check there now because she's taken the keys," Helen's unease was palpable.

"Please love, just calm it," I put my arms round her shoulders. After a moment she relaxed a little.

"I just have a bad feeling about this, that's all," she said.

"I know, but we'll be okay." My re-assurance didn't seem to comfort her. I left to find Millie.

Downstairs appeared to be deserted. I called out to Millie, but there was no reply. The lights were out in the dining room, lounge and office behind the hatch reception counter. Only the hall light remained on. The place seemed eerily still. I had no idea where Millie stayed.

I walked down the hallway to the kitchen. The door was half-open, but the light was off there too. The throbbing hum of the fridge the only sound to be heard. I made my way back to our new room.

Reaching the top of the stairway, I saw a young man and woman standing outside the room door on the left of the landing.

"Hello. Have you had a good day?" asked the man.

"Yes," I replied, surprised to see them and unaware there were any other guests in the house. "I'm planning to move on with my wife tomorrow though."

"Millie won't let you go," the woman smiled. The couple turned to enter the room and disappeared into thin air through the door. I stood there shocked. My heart starting to pump furiously. I'd just seen two ghosts. Helen was right. The place *was* haunted.

I continued standing there, desperately trying to convince myself I'd imagined the encounter, staring at the door the couple had evaporated into. Walking across, I tried the door handle. It was locked. No living entity could have entered unhindered.

The woman's words 'Millie won't let you go' echoed in my mind. It sounded doom laden. An inescapable fate. What did she mean? How could Millie prevent us leaving? Why would she want us to remain here?

I entered our room. Helen had undressed and was climbing into bed. I decided not to tell her what I'd seen on the landing. It would only worry her.

"Did you ask Millie about our phones?" she asked.

"Couldn't find her. She wasn't downstairs," I began to undress. "I'll ask her in the morning at breakfast."

"You're looking troubled," said Helen. "A bit pale. Anything wrong?"

I felt unsettled about what I'd witnessed on the landing, but played it down.

"Just tired. Need some rest." Getting into bed I turned out the bedside light, plunging the windowless, airless room in total darkness. Neither of us were in the mood for lovemaking. Sleep didn't come easily either.

Only in the early hours did I fall into a proper slumber. Even then it didn't last. As I lay on my side, I was woken by the sound of a key turning in the lock of the room door facing me. It opened and a man entered. I froze. He looked at me. Even in the darkness I could see him clearly. A young man in yellow T-shirt and jeans.

"Sorry," he said. "Didn't realise the room was occupied. You must be Millie's latest guests. I expect we'll be seeing more of each other soon." He left, re-locking the door.

"What's the matter?"

Next moment I was aware of Helen switching on her bedside light and leaning over me.

"You've been rolling over and mumbling like a maniac," she said.

It was an amazing relief to realise I must have been dreaming when I'd seen someone coming into the room. The vivid sensation of seeing another spirit.

"I'm okay, just some silly dream," I assured Helen. She looked worried.

"I don't like the pitch dark. I'm leaving the bedside light on," she said, settling back on the bed.

Proper sleep evaded me for the rest of the night, as I lay wondering whether I'd really dreamed of the man entering the room, or if I'd actually seen another ghost.

******

WEARY from a largely sleepless night, we made our way downstairs to breakfast, uplifted only by the prospect of soon being on our way from the place.

Millie greeted us with a cheery smile, placing our pot of coffee on the table.

"I hope the room was okay for you," she said. Since we'd be leaving shortly, I told her it was fine. There was no need to make a fuss about our uncomfortable night or my strange encounter on the landing.

"We can't find our phones," said Helen. "Did you see them when you moved our things?"

Millie looked puzzled.

"No," she replied. "I didn't see any phones. Are you sure you've checked through everything?"

We both nodded.

"Well I'll have another look in your old room, but I'm sure I removed all your possessions."

Ten minutes later Millie returned with our breakfasts.

"I've had a good look in your old room, but can't find any phones," she reported. "If I find them after you've left I'll send them on to your address."

"She's lying," whispered Helen when Millie returned to the kitchen.

"Why should she lie?" I couldn't see the point of Millie wanting our phones.

"I don't know, but let's get out of here as soon as we can. Hurry up and finish eating."

After breakfast we collected our luggage from the room and made our way downstairs. Millie was waiting in the hall to bid us farewell.

"How much do we owe you?" I asked.

"Oh that's alright. No charge. I've enjoyed your company. It's lonely being here on your own most of the time," Millie smiled.

"I insist we pay you something," I felt uncomfortable not paying for our stay.

"No. I don't want your money."

I took out my wallet and removed a good sum that would probably cover our costs, thrusting it towards her. Millie refused to take it. I placed it on a small side table in the hallway nearby.

"I really don't need your money. My husband left me well provided for," Millie was determined not to accept payment.

"Come on, let's get on our way," Helen tugged my arm.

Millie followed us to the car and stood watching as we loaded our bags in the boot. Climbing into our seats, I turned the key to start the engine. It whirred, but wouldn't start. After several more attempts to fruitlessly fire it into life, I got out and opened the bonnet to see what was wrong.

As I leaned inside, Millie drew near.

"The spark plugs are missing," she said.

"What? How do you know?" I began to feel anxious.

"I asked my grandson to remove them last night," Millie calmly answered.

"Why?" Now I began feeling a sense of dread. The vision of that woman on the landing I'd seen last night flashed into my head, her words 'Millie won't let you go'.

"This is ridiculous. Why did you get your grandson to remove the plugs?" My growing anxiety was turning to anger.

"Because I want both of you to stay," Millie replied, devoid of any emotion in her voice.

"What's the problem?" Helen exited the car to join me.

"She's bloody well got her grandson to remove the spark plugs," I shouted. "She's wants to keep us here. The woman's loony."

"I told you there was something weird about her," Helen gave Millie a thunderous stare. "Get your grandson to put them back," she demanded.

"He's not here, and I don't want him to put them back." Her totally calm, unmoved manner became all the more infuriating

"Right, we'll leave here on foot and get someone to fix our car. And hopefully get the police to arrest you for attempting to kidnap us." Helen's fury outmatched even mine. "You're a nutcase!"

We strode across the gravel towards the wrought iron gate. I reached to open the latch and saw a padlocked chain wrapped around the bars preventing us from leaving.

"What the hell are you playing at?" I shouted at Millie, who remained standing beside the car, smiling. It was obvious we were getting nowhere with her.

I turned back studying the gate. It was about fifteen feet high. The brick wall stretching away each side stood about three feet higher.

"It'll be a bit of a struggle, but I reckon we could climb over the gate," I said to Helen.

She surveyed the barrier and concluded that was probably our only option. With no phones to contact anyone outside, self-initiative had to be our way forward.

We gripped the bars to begin climbing. Next moment we heard fast pacing across the gravel. Millie's alsatians suddenly appeared racing towards us barking loudly.

"Stay!" Millie commanded them. The dogs immediately obeyed, sitting down and staring at us, waiting for their next instruction. Helen and me were only a couple feet into our climb.

"Now get down from there," Millie approached, "otherwise I'll have to set the dogs on you, even if you do manage to get outside. And I'd hate to spoil your young, unblemished bodies."

The thought of having the dogs tearing into us was not desirable. We jumped down.

"Why are you doing this?" Helen's anger had changed into pleading frustration..

"You'll find out," Millie replied. "I'm waiting for a delivery. Not quite sure when it will arrive."

"What delivery?" I asked.

"Can't say just yet. I'll let you know when it arrives."

"This woman really is around the twist," Helen whispered.

"For now I'd like you to return to your room," Millie's calm manner persisted, that smile, though for the first time her eyes no longer held the accompanying warmth. Their depths seemed distant, harbouring an unspoken fate for us.

"Let's do as she asks for the moment," I whispered to Helen, "and work a way out of this."

My wife's expression was grim, harbouring thoughts of vengeance, but without saying anything I could tell she agreed with me to bide our time. Wait for the right opportunity to act.

We walked back to the house followed by Millie with her two alsatians aside her like guards ensuring the prisoners remained in line. We felt humiliated, but with no other option other than to play the part for now, and not risk being ripped apart by the dogs.

We were shepherded back to the room we'd been moved into, and it began to dawn on us that there had likely been no problem with our first room. That there was no water leakage and Millie had made up the story to transfer us into her windowless prison. God knows for what reason.

"What you're doing is illegal, holding us against our will," Helen protested as we entered the room with the dogs watchfully accompanying Millie. Our host, now our warder, said nothing as she closed the door behind us and turned the key in the lock.

"Because you've behaved badly, there'll be no food for you for the rest of the day," Millie called from outside. Her condescending attitude infuriated me.

I shoulder charged the door to break it open. It didn't budge. The wood was solid. The lock firm. Several times I tried to break through it, booting, shouldering again. Still the barrier refused to budge.

"Stop wasting your energy," said Helen, now sitting on the side of the bed. "She's obviously made sure this is a very secure room."

I sat down beside Helen on the bed, gripping my forehead.

"How the hell did we get into this situation?" a feeling of hopelessness flooded through me.

"More to the point what situation are we in?" wondered Helen. "Millie seems to have something in mind for us. What did she mean waiting for a delivery?"

"Heaven knows, but we've got to find a way out." I looked around for an opportunity to escape. Something to break through or open as an exit. There was a narrow recess in the wall.

"Looks like that used to be a window," I said, rapping it with my knuckles. "It's been bricked in and wallpapered over. She's turned the room into a prison." Then the same dark thoughts came into our minds.

"The ghost I saw," Helen's eyes widened.

"I saw ghosts too," I confessed to her, "outside a room door on this landing."

"You never told me," she stared accusingly.

"I didn't want to worry you."

"Did Millie trap them in here too while they were alive?" Helen conjectured. "Guests on walking holidays?"

I was thinking on the same lines.

"Did she offer them accommodation like us too? Unhappy with where they were staying, or just calling in on the off-chance?" I continued the thinking.

The theory on the face of it seemed ludicrous, but neither of us could escape the conclusion that we were now in a holding place, waiting for this mysterious delivery of Millie's.

The theory also led us to another horrific conclusion. Our death would be the result, condemned to join the un-dead spirits that roamed this house.

We were silent for a while, our minds racing to contend with what seemed a far fetched idea on the one hand, but strangely feasible on the other.

"No, there must be some other explanation," I pushed away from dark thoughts. "We're letting our imaginations run away with us." We silently considered our position again for a little longer.

"Maybe we are running away with strange ideas," Helen agreed. "But one thing is certain. We have to find a way to escape from the mad woman."

CHAPTER 4

OUR imprisonment in the room even for a few hours felt unending. Fortunately we had our backpacks with us containing a few snack bars and soft drinks. It was the only nourishment we would get that day.

The thought of being stuck in the room for heaven knows how long began to fray our nerves.

"I told you we should have left sooner," Helen sniped at me.

"How was I to know the woman was a loony?" I shot back.

For a long time we said nothing, harbouring regrets at starting to fall out with each other and fearing what fate Millie had in store for us.

I remembered I had a penknife and tried to pick the keyhole door lock with some of the attachments. All attempts were futile. We rested on the bed as the hours ticked away. With just the room light on, we could only tell it was evening by our watches.

"I'm going to take a shower," Helen announced, starting to undress.

"We've got one snack bar left for dinner," I said, trying to maintain our sanity with a light and probably stupid remark.

"We're the fucking prisoners of a nutcase, and you're trying to have a laugh," Helen sneered. Now naked, she stormed off into the en-suite slamming the door behind her.

I sat on the side of the bed, desperately trying to think of a way to escape, when the en-suite door flew open and Helen came racing out in terror.

"There's a man in the shower," she yelled.

"What?" I sprang up and tore in. There was no man present and the shower wasn't running. I came out and told Helen.

"It's another fucking ghost, isn't it. God knows I'm going to go mad in this place." Her face was drawn, tearful. She slumped, sitting on the bedside.

"I'll find a way out," I promised, with as yet no idea how. But I wanted to give her a sense of hope.

Ditching the idea of showering, she climbed into bed, burying herself under the quilt. A couple of minutes later the room light went out and we were plunged into complete darkness. Millie it seemed had cut off our power supply, deciding it was time for us to rest.

I undressed in the pitch black and snuggled up to Helen. She remained rigid, not responding even to just cuddle together.

******

NEITHER of us really slept that night. Only shallow rest. Occasionally I heard Helen mumbling something incoherently, suggesting she was in some sort of slumber.

What time it was I had no idea. Or whether I was dreaming or not. But suddenly I sat up with a start, thinking I'd seen a face in the darkness staring down at me from the ceiling.

46

"What's the matter?" Helen sprang up in panic.

"Nothing, nothing," I said, not wanting to terrify her. She settled back again and I laid down, only this time on my side, so that I wasn't facing the ceiling.

As I lay awake for what seemed an eternity, the room light came on. Glancing at my watch it showed seven-thirty. I presumed it was morning, having no daylight in this windowless room to gauge natural day and night.

"Millie's decided to let us see again," said Helen, sitting up in the bed. There was a knock at the door.

"If you behave yourselves, I'll let you out of the room in half-an-hour and give you breakfast," Millie called through the door.

"I don't feel like eating," Helen said to me, shaking her head wearily.

"We've got to eat," I told her. "We need to keep our strength up if we're going to work a way out of here."

"Do you promise to behave?" Millie called again.

"Yes," I called back, infuriated at the woman treating us like naughty schoolchildren, but reigning in my instinct of telling her to fuck off.

We dressed and washed, Helen insisting I stood by the open en-suite door while she was in there, in case another visitation occured.

A key turned in the lock and Millie opened the door, her dogs, Rufus and Petra, standing by her side eyeing us war-ily. Our warders followed us downstairs into the dining room where a table was laid for our breakfast. Millie departed to fetch the meals while the dogs remained with us watchfully on guard.

She returned with a fry-up that was my favourite, and scrambled egg with smoked salmon that had been Helen's first choice on our arrival.

"Why are you doing this to us, holding us prisoner?" I pleaded, hoping I might appeal to a reasonable side of Millie's nature.

"You aren't prisoners. You're free to roam the grounds, the house, if you just respect my wishes for you to stay here," she smiled, convinced that she'd given a perfectly reasonable explanation.

"This place is haunted, isn't it?" Helen aimed directly.

"Oh, I wouldn't say that," Millie replied without hesitation. "I enjoy the company of my young guests. Makes me feel younger." She turned, sweeping her arm to indicate the other tables in the room.

"They're all enjoying their breakfasts. Young walkers like yourselves, who've called in for accommodation over the years," Millie said proudly. "They all decided to stay, but just like you, reluctantly at first. Now they're all happy."

The other tables were unlaid. No-one sat at them. Was Millie deluded? Or did she see people there? Spirits? Young hikers who had stayed here and were now dead?

We'd had little appetite to start with for the breakfast, now as she left the room it completely disappeared.

"She's murdered her guests," Helen looked terrified.

"We don't know that," I tried to play it down to stop us both descending into horrified wrecks. But like Helen, I feared as much.

"The ghosts we've seen have all been young, about our age," Helen began to shake.

"Get a grip. Panic won't get us out of here. Play Millie along. We need to find a weak spot in the place," I reached across the table and held her hand.

"Now eat. Force it down if necessary. We need to keep our strength up."

******

SITTING at the terrace table in the back garden with soft drinks provided by Millie could have been heavenly, were it not for our impending sense of doom.

The alsatians rested on their haunches with keen eyes on us, acting as a stark reminder we were still prisoners, despite this partial freedom allowed by our unhinged host. Millie had even granted us the right to wander the grounds and permissible guest areas of the house, after we'd made the promise at breakfast to behave ourselves.

Given these limited privileges, we spent time looking around the setting for possible ways of escape. The high brick wall completely surrounding the property didn't help.

A tall tree not far from the chalet at the far end of the enclosure had sturdy lower branches that Helen and me were capable of stretching up to reach.

If we were quick, we could distance ourselves from the dogs' vicious clutches and climb it. A higher branch pointed level with the top of the wall, but there was a ten foot gap between. A leap of six feet we'd be prepared to risk. Ten would require us to have wings. And, of course, a drop of nearly twenty feet on the other side also risked serious injury or worse.

As the day progressed Millie gave us lunch and an evening meal, carrying on as if we were guests on a perfectly normal holiday. It gave us the creepy sensation of being fattened up by the wicked witch in Hansel and Gretel, preparing us for a grisly fate.

"You must stay healthy," she said, as she served our evening meal in the dining room. "My other guests are enjoying their meals," again she indicated the other empty tables in the dining room. Still we could see no-one at them, but had the uneasy feeling spirits were present that for now only Millie could see.

We had little appetite, but were determined to eat just enough to keep surviving the ordeal. After the meal we took another stroll to the tree near the chalet to consider again the option of using it to escape, the dogs continually tracking our every movement.

"Maybe we could knot the bed sheets and tie one end to the top branch, and use it to swing across to the wall," Helen suggested.

"Then jump twenty feet to the ground?" I dismissed the idea.

"Might be bushes on the other side to give us a softish landing," she speculated.

"Or our broken bones if there aren't. Even if we did succeed, Millie would set the dogs to find us. You know how good they are at tracking."

I wanted to believe Helen's idea could be done, but the place was like a fortress. There had to be another way, not necessarily without risk, but hopefully less risky.

We began to walk back to the house and saw a young couple standing on the chalet veranda staring at us. They wore short sleeved tops and shorts.

"Lovely evening," the woman called to us. Both of them looked fully like living flesh and blood.

"Come far?" asked the man. Helen and I were confused. Had Millie taken in new lodgers? The two seemed so real. Hardly like ghosts.

"I expect you'll be joining us here soon," the woman didn't wait for a reply to her partner's question. "Would you like to see inside?" The couple approached the chalet door and evaporated through it.

We stood there unable to move for a moment. They were ghosts we'd seen. The whole place seemed to be filled with spectral residents.

"God, we've really got to get out of here," Helen took my arm.

"What's inside the chalet?" I wondered. "I'm going to see if the door is unlocked."

""Be careful," Helen released me and I mounted the short flight of steps on to the veranda. The door was locked. I pushed it hard with the palm of my hand, just in case it was jammed shut, but still it wouldn't budge. I heard growling from behind. The alsatians who'd been watching our every move were now approaching, sending the message to move away from the door.

Wishing to stay in one piece I obeyed, and descended the steps back on to the lawn. The animals calmed down, but remained vigilant, following closely as we returned to the house.

51

******

FOR the next few days our routine followed the same pattern. Locked in our room at night with no light, and allowed to wander the grounds in the daytime with access to some of the downstairs rooms.

Mercifully, apart from strange whispering that sometimes woke me from the sparse sleep I could get in the night, we hadn't seen any more spirit manifestations.

In between our so far fruitless attempts to hatch an effective escape plan, an opportunity suddenly presented itself while we were in the sitting room with glasses of soft drinks, quietly discussing various ways.

"Maybe if I sneak some breakfast bacon out and throw it to the dogs when we're on the forecourt, it might distract them for a moment so we can climb over the gate," I whispered to Helen.

"But you said the other day Millie would probably set the dogs to track us the minute we get outside," Helen reminded me.

"Yes, but I remember there's a cottage about half-a-mile away. If we're quick we could get to it and alert the owners." I knew as I spoke, Helen wasn't overly convinced with the idea.

As that plan crumbled to dust, from the open window overlooking the forecourt we heard the sound of a van pulling up outside the gate. I looked out. It was a post van.

A man exited and opened the back doors taking out a small parcel. Then he pressed the bell button in the side wall. We weren't sure where Millie was at that moment and the dogs, unusually, were not keeping us under guard.

A plan was rapidly forming in my mind as we heard Millie approaching from somewhere in the house and making her way down the hallway to open the front door. She left and I saw her cross the forecourt to unlock the chain round the gate.

"High security?" I heard the postman query, wondering why there was a locked chain in place.

"Had someone trying to break in," Millie lied while unlocking it. "Just a precaution for now." She opened the gate to take the package.

"Hold on," I called to Helen, and rushed from the room down the hallway shouting 'help, we're being held hostage!'

I'd just about reached the open front door to run outside and call for help again, when the alsatians leapt at me from behind, barging me flat on my face. They jumped over me and sprang out the doorway racing towards the gate.

I looked up. The postman was terrified seeing the dogs racing towards him. Swiftly he rushed back to his van and pulled away. The animals calmed down and stood obediently by Millie as she locked the chain around the gate bars. My cry for help was in vain.

Millie approached with the dogs by her side, as I got up and Helen joined me.

"That was a very silly thing to do," Millie admonished me. "Now I will have to confine you both to your room and serve you meals on a tray."

I glanced at the package she held. Millie seemed to read my mind.

"No, this is not the delivery that will let me proceed on my business with you. For that we will have to wait a little longer."

At that moment I was tempted to grab the woman and wrest the chain key off her. But the dogs beside their mistress made me think otherwise.

"Don't worry," Millie smiled that devious smile. "I shall send my other guests to keep you company from time to time."

We were herded back to that damned prison room, feeling more trapped and isolated than ever, now certain that Millie's house and grounds were inhabited by the ghosts of former guests she'd murdered. And that we were the next on the list to join them.

Our horror of confinement grew deeper. The room light was now cut off an hour earlier at eight every night, plunging us into a longer period of terrifying manifestations in the total darkness. Frequently we heard the sound of a spirit showering in the en-suite, then saw spectres of couples wandering through the door into the room and disappearing through a sidewall.

They carried on as if we didn't exist, except one bearded man who stood beside our bed one night with a rucksack on his back.

"Don't worry too much," he said, "Millie will murder you perfectly without pain." Then he dissolved into the darkness. Our terror deepened at the dreadful fate awaiting us. We desperately needed to escape. But how?

The room light came on again at seven-thirty every morning. Millie, with her dogs carefully guarding her, brought in meals on a tray. Our appetites, however, were fading like the chances of escape. Every time she arrived, we feared she would announce the delivery she was waiting on had come, spelling our imminent demise. The tension was driving us insane, and we took again to arguing over whose fault it was that had brought us into this misery.

"You wanted to go on a hiking holiday," I'd say to Helen.

"You didn't leave here when I said we should," she struck back.

Then we would hug each other, knowing that arguing was pointless. Neither of us could have guessed we'd encounter a psychopath whose house was filled with the ghosts of people she'd murdered.

We resolved to keep a grip on our senses, going through some of Helen's keep fit exercise routines, telling each other stories of our childhoods, even playing I-Spy, anything to stop our minds descending into deep depression. At times, in frustration, I'd again attempt to barge the door down, only to be met by growling and barking on the other side.

Gradually the routine of lights on, lights off, and sudden terrifying spectral visits in the darkness wore down our morale. We began to spend more time in a stupor of sleep to escape the reality of our seemingly hopeless situation. Insanity could arrive sooner than Millie's special delivery.

CHAPTER 5

JULIA relaxed on the living room sofa at her two-bedroom flat in Belhaven, watching her favourite TV cookery show.

She held a mug of coffee and was laughing as the man in the show competing with other amateur cooks, suddenly recoiled as a dollop of cream in a mixer flew out and splatted on his nose.

Her phone rang. She placed the mug on the nearby coffee table and muted the TV.

"Hope I'm not disturbing your evening's viewing, but just wondered if you'd heard from Helen?" the woman calling asked.

"Not lately Diane. Why should I have done?" Julia replied.

"It's just that she hasn't turned up for work at the gym. Not for a week now. Wondering what's happened to her?"

Diane worked at the same gym as Julia's sister-in-law, Helen. They all got on well together, and Julia living only about fifteen miles away from their homes in Birmingham, would meet them for girls' nights out.

"Haven't heard from my brother Andrew lately either," said Julia. "But he's not the best one for keeping in touch. You know what blokes are like."

"Yes, I do," Diane replied mournfully, reflecting on the edgy relationship she was currently going through. On that front they were soul sisters. Julia's partner had abruptly left the flat they shared six months earlier, taking up with another woman.

"I'm a bit worried. Helen is very reliable, and isn't someone not to turn up for work without a word," Diane expressed her concern.

"I spoke to Andrew about a fortnight ago when they were on holiday in the Yorkshire Dales, but the phone cut off," explained Julia. "Tried calling him back a few times, but couldn't get a reply. I thought they were probably in a place where the signal was unreliable."

"I've tried Helen's phone, but that just goes to messaging," said Diane. "Haven't got Andrew's number."

"Leave it with me. I'll give him a ring. Find out what's going on."

"Thanks," Diane replied. "Speak soon."

Julia called her brother's phone. It went through to messaging. She left a message asking him to call back and continued watching TV.

By noon the next day, Andrew still hadn't rung. Sitting in the rest room during her one o'clock lunch break at the textile company office where she worked, Julia called her brother again. Still only the messaging service.

Like Diane, she was now beginning to worry. Andrew wasn't the best communicator, but this now seemed overly long for a reply.

She rang Helen's number, which also switched to messaging. Julia left a message, though resolved if she hadn't heard back from them by the end of the day, she'd take the twenty minute drive to their home to see if they were there. Unusual it might be, but both their phones could possibly be out of order, or battery power at the same time she decided. Whichever, they should have returned home from holiday by now.

That evening Julia parked outside the block of apartments where her brother and Helen lived and took the lift to the sixth floor.

Receiving no answer to the doorbell, she let herself in with the key Andrew had given her to keep as a spare in case he and Helen lost theirs.

The rooms seemed eerily quiet. She had only ever visited when they were at home. Without their presence the atmosphere felt strangely lonely. Julia's concern for the couple deepened.

She left the apartment and drove home, trying to convince herself there was a perfectly reasonable explanation as to why they hadn't returned, but it didn't allay her growing fear that something awful might have happened to them. Back in her flat, watching the TV did nothing to drive out the fear.

Andrew had told her that he and Helen were staying at a place called Sunnyside in the Yorkshire Dales. The problem was that the Dales covered a large area and she couldn't remember which part.

She searched on her laptop for accommodation called Sunnyside in the locality. It displayed five places with the same name. Which one was it? Then she saw Carnswold village beside one of them. It instantly rang a bell. Andrew had mentioned that name to her before leaving on holiday.

Julia called the phone number given.

"Yes?" a woman answered sourly.

"I'm trying to contact my brother Andrew Swanson," said Julia. "He was staying at your place with his wife Helen about a couple of weeks ago. They seem to be missing and I was wondering if you know where they could be?"

Next moment the line cut off. Julia redialed several times, but the line remained engaged.

Then it came to her that when she'd called Andrew on holiday, he'd said Sunnyside was no good. From the rude reception she'd received, she could understand why.

More of that conversation flowed back to her. He said they'd moved to another place. Something about a grand old house, tall wrought iron gate and some high walls. The phone line had been scratchy and indistinct. Andrew hadn't said where it was before the signal cut out.

Julia went to the kitchen to make herself a cup of coffee, still struggling in her mind to try and recall any other clues. She was sure he'd said the place was not far away from Sunnyside.

Then another dreadful thought came to her. If something terrible had happened to them, she should first check with the local police for that area. She looked up the number on her laptop and rang, fearing some awful news.

The call taker left her on hold for some time to check, increasing Julia's concern. It was a great relief when she was told no incidents relating to Andrew or Helen had been recorded, but it took her no further forward.

She decided to give it another day to hear from them, leaving messages on both their phones.

At work next day, not having received a reply from either of them, her mind was unable to concentrate on the job at hand. Nagging worry that maybe their car had gone off the road and ended up in a deep ditch down an embankment haunted her mind. They might be laying trapped or injured in the vehicle, possibly even dying, unheard or seen by passing traffic. She'd seen stories like that.

As the morning wore on, plagued by even more imaginations of them suffering a dire fate, she resolved that she'd have to travel to the Yorkshire Dales and try to track them down.

At lunchtime she decided to make one more check, ringing the main hospital in the area where they'd gone on holiday. That too produced no result.

Later in the day Julia spoke to her office manager to ask if she could take a few days holiday leave, outlining her worry. John Hallet was a kindly man in his mid-fifties, sympathetic to her concern and granted her the time off.

"Don't worry though, things usually turn out okay," he said encouragingly, as she left the office. Julia sincerely hoped so.

******

THAT evening she packed a few clothes and toiletries, and called Andrew and Helen's numbers again, hoping for a reply. None came.

She had no idea precisely where to look for them other than to try and find the place Andrew had briefly described. A grand old house, tall wrought iron gate and high walls. A few miles away from Sunnyside, she thought she remembered him saying.

But did he mean three, five, seven, eight? That could be a lot of area to travel in the winding roads and narrow lanes criss-crossing the Dales setting. She'd checked the online map. And had they stayed there long, or moved to somewhere else? Then the dread thought returned. Were they trapped in a ditch down a deep embankment?

For a starting point, early next morning Julia headed on the long journey to Carnswold village, the first location where Andrew and Helen had stayed.

If she worked her way round the roads from there in a radius of a few miles or more, she might come across the property Andrew had described. Whoever lived there could hopefully give her more information as to where they'd gone.

Arriving in Carnswold just after midday, she pulled into a parking bay close to the village cafe. She went inside for a sandwich and coffee before travelling the local roads.

"Here on holiday?" the young woman behind the counter greeted her. It was the question she posed to anyone who looked like a visiting stranger.

"No," Julia replied.

"Business then?" the woman asked, removing the packaged sandwich Julia had ordered from the glass fronted unit on the counter, and placing it on a plate. Julia shook her head to the question.

The thought crossed her mind that perhaps Andrew and Helen may well have come to the cafe for a coffee while they'd been in the village.

"My brother and his wife stayed in this village on holiday just over a fortnight ago. They seem to have gone missing," Julia related her tale, giving their names. The cafe owner's interest piqued.

Julia had a photo of the couple stored on her phone and showed it to the woman.

"Do you recognise them?"

The cafe assistant studied it for a moment.

"We get a lot of people in here," she said. " I don't re-member them all. But I do vaguely remember those faces."

"Did they ever say anything to you? Mention places they were staying or going to?" Julia clutched at hope.

"Not that I recall," the woman replied.

Julia replaced the phone in her bag and paid for her pur-chase. Another thought came to mind.

"Is there an old house with a tall wrought iron gate and high wall anywhere near here?"

The woman considered Julia's question, then shook her head.

"Sorry, nothing comes to me, but there's lots of cottages and houses tucked away down small roads and tracks in the Dales. Could be anywhere," came the unhelpful reply.

Julia took the tray containing her sandwich and coffee to find a table, suddenly aware that she'd become the whis-pered focus of attention by other seated customers.

Feeling uncomfortably out of place in this unfamiliar setting, she quickly consumed her lunch and left the premises to start her search.

The scenic road views over hills, through pastures and quaint villages, all ideal to calm the spirit, were wasted on her as she concentrated solely on trying to find the house of

Andrew's vague description. Mile after mile Julia searched, but the needle in this haystack remained hidden.

As the day drew to a close and proving to be fruitless, she had the choice of just returning home or doggedly continuing the search next day.

Checking on her phone for local accommodation, the town of Alcott seemed to offer the widest range and was nearby. She drove there and checked into a hotel. It wasn't top quality, but luxury accommodation was not high on her list of priorities.

The following day she continued her trawl of local roads and narrow lanes, some even deteriorating into unmade tracks where two cars could hardly pass each other.

In late afternoon, without any food or drink since early breakfast, a sense of complete hopelessness began to drain her spirit. She'd emerged from a narrow track road that had led to yet another isolated property not fitting Andrew's description. The fear of never seeing her brother and his wife ever again terrified her. She was now convinced something dreadful had happened to them.

She stopped the car in a small layby and reached for her handbag on the passenger seat, taking out a tissue to wipe away tears in her eyes.

"Are you alright my dear?" asked an elderly grey-bearded man, wearing a green puffer coat and Panama hat, craning at the open car window. "Have you lost your way? It's easy to do that in these parts."

The man's comforting voice put Julia at ease and she felt silly being seen wiping tears from her eyes. She noticed he was holding a lead with a golden retriever at the end of it gazing up at her.

"Beautiful dog," she said. The man smiled

"She is, isn't she. I'm just taking my Sheba for a walk." He stooped and patted the dog's head, then turned back to Julia.

"But are you alright? Forgive me for saying, but you look a little upset," he gazed at her sympathetically.

"No, I'm okay," Julia played down her plight, not wanting to burden him with her woes. She paused, and the man prepared to walk on, deciding that whatever troubled the woman he didn't want to pry into her private affairs.

"But you might be able to help me," Julia called as he started to move on. He stopped. She gave him the scant description of the place she was looking for.

"Ah, sounds like Longhurst House," said the man. "Yes, Millie Hendry lives there. Nice woman. The house is about five miles away. Off the beaten track. You have to go down several narrow lanes to reach it by road. Not always easy to find unless you're local or someone tells you."

Huge relief swept through Julia. She wanted to get out of the car and hug the man.

"Have you a pen and some paper?" he asked. "Be best if I drew you a small map." Julia took a biro and notebook from her handbag. The man made a diagram resting the notebook on the roof. Julia wasn't a great map reader, but his illustration was surprisingly clear.

"Thank you so much," she smiled at him. The man seemed puzzled as to why a simple bit of help seemed to have made her look so relieved. He raised his hat to her in acknowledgment and continued walking with his dog.

******

HOW much stress it takes to go completely insane, I had no idea. But Helen and I felt sure we were nearing that point.

In the depths of hell to which we'd been plunged, it was becoming impossible to think straight anymore. Night and day no longer existed in our airless, walled prison beyond the routine of the room light going off at eight and returning at seven-thirty, when Millie would enter under guard dog protection to serve us breakfast on a tray. Though we hardly touched that now.

Everything in our minds was merging into an endless stream, growing barely aware of beginnings and ends as our morale gradually declined further. I-Spy games, recounting childhood memories, imagining what we'd do if we won a fortune on the lottery, and other distractions from our trap, became harder for us to concentrate on.

But worse than imprisonment was the increasing number of terrifying spectral visitations in the long hours of total darkness. Disembodied laughing and screaming. Ghostly couples walking in and out of the room through the door and walls. Spirits materialising beside our beds and staring at us curiously before disappearing again.

Our only hope was that when people realised we hadn't returned home, they'd begin a search. The big downside to that theory was the fact no-one would know precisely where we were. We'd left no word at Sunnyside about our next destination, and I didn't tell my sister Julia our new location before the phone signal cut out. The line was also faint, so I wasn't sure she'd heard much of anything I'd said.

I laid awake on the bed beside Helen in that damned period of total darkness, the thoughts racing through my mind. Resting on my back, that face suddenly appeared again, staring at me from the ceiling. A young man with a pitying look in his eyes, as if he knew the fate awaiting us.

"Go away!" I shouted, startling Helen. The face disappeared.

"What's the matter?" Julia sprang up. "I was just managing to get a snatch of rest," she groaned.

"I'm sorry. It's nothing, just a dream," I lied, placing my arm round her, not wishing to cause her any more distress by telling her what I'd seen.

It was gradually destroying me to witness Helen's state of mind slowly being eroded by that monster, Millie, imprisoning us. I wanted to kill the woman. My hatred for her grew more intense. If only a moment would present itself when she was unguarded.

I'd thought about the risk of being attacked by the dogs in an effort for us to escape, but if they ripped Helen and me to pieces it would hardly be a victory. And without being freed from confinement in this prison, there was no scope to attempt a way out.

The room darkness suddenly disappeared as the light came on, indicating another day had begun. Which day and week seemed to no longer have any relevance.

We heard the key turn in the door lock and once again Millie appeared carrying a tray with our breakfasts, the warder alsatians standing alert outside.

"Come on," she said with a cheery smile," you must eat. You won't be any good for my purpose looking pale and unhealthy." She placed the tray on the dresser as we sat up on the bed, fully clothed and unwashed, having no desire or reason to be presentable to the world anymore.

"The delivery I've been waiting for will be arriving soon, and I need you to be ready for it," Millie announced in a tone of joyful anticipation. The sight of bacon, eggs, sausages and fried tomato on the breakfast plate, that once would have made my mouth water, no longer enticed me. Fresh fruit and yogurt for Helen had also lost its appeal. Lethargy was turning us into mindless zombies.

"I'm taking you out for a walk round the grounds today," Millie smiled that smile to which anyone not knowing her would be fooled into thinking she was a kindly old lady. But we could now see the devious evil that resided within.

After she left, we picked at the food more to try and sustain strength than satisfy hunger. A short time later Millie returned and tutted at us for not eating much.

"Come on, let's get you outside," she said. "Some fresh air and exercise will help to sharpen your appetite and restore the colour in your cheeks."

Her dogs herded us down the stairs and along the corridor, through the back door into the garden. The smell of fresh air was vitalisingly sweet. The sunlight warmed our souls.

Millie guided us along the garden to the far end and on to the lawn area in front of the chalet.

"Won't be too long now when I'll be able to show you the beautiful things I store in there," she said, looking towards the wooden structure. Something in her tone seemed to veil menace, and gave us the feeling that whatever beautiful things she thought lay inside there, would not turn out to be our idea of beauty.

"Walk round the lawn," Millie ordered, the dogs keeping a close eye to ensure we obeyed. Strangely, even under this duress, we actually enjoyed the limited freedom in open air.

Maybe five minutes had passed when the ears of Rufus and Petra pricked up. They began growling and barking.

"What's the matter?" Millie asked them. They started moving towards the branches which overhung the path leading back to the house.

"Someone coming?"

The dogs barked to confirm a visitor was nearby.

"Right, get back inside," Millie commanded, the animals ensuring we complied with the order. We were ushered into the house as the gate bell rang in the hallway. It rang again as she hurried us upstairs back to our prison.

******

MILLIE saw a young woman dressed in a dark red, knee-length dress standing outside the gate and a car parked on the other side of the road.

"Yes, can I help you?" she asked, standing behind the wrought iron bars.

"Sorry to trouble you," said Julia, "but I'm looking for my brother Andrew Swanson and his wife Helen. Last time I spoke to him on the phone, he said that they were staying in a place that matches yours."

Millie felt alarmed that a relative was virtually on the doorstep searching for the couple she held captive. But she skilfully put on that benign smile, pondering thoughtfully for a moment as if trying to recall a memory.

"Of course, forgive me. I'm sometimes forgetful at my age," she said, after going through the motion of remembering something.

"Come inside." Millie unlocked the chain around the gate. "And sorry for the high security, but there have been break-ins in the area recently and I'm just taking this precaution." She opened the gate. Her alsatians sat keenly watching by the front door of the house as Julia entered the grounds.

"Yes, they stayed here for a night," she paused, pretending to recall further. "Must have been about a couple of weeks ago now. Then they decided to move on."

"Did they say where they were going?" Julia clung to the hope she'd found a positive lead.

Millie feigned a memory recall act again.

"No, they didn't say where they were going next."

Julia's hope dissolved into deep disappointment.

"Are you certain?" she pressed. Millie nodded.

"You live in a beautiful place," Julia complimented. "I can see why my brother and Helen would have stopped here."

"Dates back a long way," Millie replied, now relaxing in the belief she'd put this meddlesome visitor off the scent.

Julia thanked her and climbed back into the car, her heart heavy that the trail had gone cold.

She returned to stay another night at the hotel in Alcott, numbed by the inability to think of another way to find Andrew and Helen. She rang their numbers yet again, only to be met by messaging.

CHAPTER 6

BACK at work a couple of days later, Julia just couldn't concentrate. Her mind continued to dwell on the missing couple.

"Do you need a little more time off?" asked her manager, John Hallet, seeing she looked drawn and depressed. "Can your family help?"

"No I'll be okay," Julia shook her head, shrugging away his concern.

She had considered telling her parents, who had moved to France after giving up their UK jobs and opted to run a restaurant in Paris. But they'd be distressed and hurry back. She'd give it a little more time before telling them.

Julia and Andrew had another brother, Phillip, but he too had moved abroad, now living in Spain with his wife. She wouldn't tell him just yet either.

Helen had fallen out with her parents some years back. They had a right to know, of course. But again, clinging to the hope something would turn up soon, Julia decided to hold off for now. How could any of them progress it any further anyway?

Julia's hope of something turning up soon was fulfilled in an unexpected way.

For several days her mind had been distracted from the reality of everyday events. A clue was trying hard to surface from somewhere deep inside. Something subliminally noted, but stuck in transmission to conscious thought.

Another restless night robbed her of healing sleep. She got out of bed and poured herself a glass of water in the kitchen.

Returning to bed, she glanced at the bedside clock. It was four in the morning. After a while, she managed to descend into a light doze.

Her dream took her to the rolling hills and valleys of the Yorkshire Dales. She was driving along narrow roads with hedgerows lining the sides.

Next moment she stood on the gravel forecourt of a grand house talking to Millie. The dream conversation was indistinct. Julia's eyes were wandering to a car parked at the side of the forecourt. A deep blue coloured car with a registration number that was indistinct, but fuzzily began AV.

She woke with a start, feeling intensely fearful. As Julia re-ran the dream in conscious recall, she remembered she'd seen a deep blue car parked on the forecourt during her visit to Millie. She was certain Andrew and Helen had a car the same colour. Julia wasn't particularly car model aware, but felt sure theirs was a Ford Fiesta.

She left the bed and went into the living room to settle on the sofa with her laptop. Then began searching through her family and friends photo albums. Julia was sure she'd taken a photo of Andrew and Helen when they'd just bought a new car, possibly two or three years earlier. She didn't give specific file names to each image, so the search was a scatter-gun approach.

After half-an-hour of loading and studying numerous images, she began to lose heart as to whether or not the photo had been saved and stored. Making herself a cup of coffee, she returned to continue the search, which was nearing the end of stored images.

A few more sprang up of smiling friendly faces, parties, restaurant dinners. Then suddenly a photo of Andrew and Helen standing beside their new car flashed on to the screen. A deep blue Ford Fiesta, with the registration plate beginning AV.

Julia's joy at finding the photo was demolished by the sensation of dread. What the hell was their car doing parked on that woman's forecourt, when she'd said her brother and Helen had left the place?

Maybe it wasn't their car. Julia's mind became clouded with doubt. After all, that make of car wasn't uncommon, and there must be others with registrations beginning AV. She struggled to recall the dream, even now fading in memory, hoping she would see a number match showing the remainder of the registration. But she drew a blank.

Still, it seemed long odds on coincidence that Millie, or someone else staying there, would have the same car model and colour beginning AV. She needed to start digging further.

She rang work at six thirty before anyone would be at the office, leaving a message saying she wouldn't be in that day. A short time later, Julia joined the town's first wave of early morning commuter traffic, and headed for the fresher pastures of the Yorkshire Dales - totally unaware of the horrific revelation to come.

******

MILLIE had wondered if Julia had noticed the Ford Fiesta still parked on the forecourt when she'd locked the gate chain and watched Andrew's interfering sister depart in her car.

The woman hadn't mentioned anything about the vehicle and didn't appear to recognise it, so Millie felt sure its presence wouldn't set off any alarm. But she reprimanded herself for not removing it sooner.

Back in the house she called her grandson Nick on the phone, telling him to come round after he'd finished work to replace the spark plugs in the vehicle, and move it into the garage set back on the forecourt.

It could stay there hidden from view for a while, and then Nick would drive it to a remote spot several miles away and set it alight with petrol, destroying any evidence that could be traced back to her. Using his bicycle stored in the car for the outward journey, Nick would then cycle home. Millie's genial exterior ran deep with cunning.

Later that evening, she sat on an armchair in a wood panelled room on the top floor of the house. The setting was dimly lit by two flickering candles perched at each end of the marble mantelpiece. On a table nearby lay an open leatherbound book.

She had just finished reading an entry in the book, and began reciting words from it that she'd memorised. Her alsatians lay resting beside her on the red carpet.

The words she recited were of an ancient foreign language. As she continued, the dogs ears pricked up, but they remained unmoved. They were familiar with the strange practices of their mistress.

A few moments later the forms of two heavily decayed bodies covered in dirt slowly materialized before her, their flesh eaten away by worms and rotted by bacteria, dark voids where eyes once looked out upon the world.

"Ruth and Michael, I just wanted to apologise to you," Millie spoke to the ghoulish apparitions as if talking to the dead was perfectly normal.

"Forgive me both, but I learned so much from you. I wanted you to know that. You helped me to perfect my art. Your lives were not wasted." She paused, smiling at them. "Now return to where I buried you."

The decayed souls vaporised into the ether.

******

THE mad woman holding us prisoner was insistent that Helen and I should take exercise outside every day, forcing us to spend time walking to the far end of the grounds, and make numerous circuits of the chalet lawn.

Millie appeared concerned about our general health, that our complexions had grown pale, which seemed odd given the unhealthy conditions of confinement we were trapped in would naturally cause our health to deteriorate.

"I only want good looking young people staying here," she said, as we continued parading round the grounds under alsatian watch. "You've seen the other young people staying here. They often pop in to have a chat with me. I do love young company."

The only young company Helen and myself ever met were ghosts, plaguing us at any time, room light on or off, night and day. Driving us to the edge of insanity.

We had just returned to our room after yet another 'health giving' walk, when we heard the shower burst into life. I sprang into the en-suite.

"Fucking get out of here!" I shouted at the naked man standing under the water spray. Through the glass door I saw him sweeping back his soaking hair and smiling at me. For a moment it appeared this was actually a living human being in the cubicle. Then he disappeared and the spray stopped. Not a droplet of water stuck to the glass partition, nor was it wet inside.

I couldn't take much more of these incessant hauntings, and Helen was reaching the end of her tolerance. She lay on the bed facing the ceiling, staring blankly. Her mind was taking her elsewhere, oblivious to the present surroundings. I just had to do something to rescue her from here, but mental exhaustion was now clouding my ability to think clearly. Like climbing a hill with your legs giving way.

I think it was a day or two later, I'd lost touch with sequences, when Millie came in beaming from ear to ear as she carried the breakfast tray.

"My special delivery has arrived," she announced. "At last I'll be able to show you what's inside the chalet."

It was an announcement that obviously thrilled her, but drove a shaft of terror through Helen and me. What diabolical fate awaited us?

"Cheer up," she said, seeing our alarmed faces, "soon you'll be free to join my other guests and wander the house and grounds happily forever. You're so lucky to remain in such a beautiful part of the country."

If Helen and I were well on the road to insanity, this woman had already arrived there.

Millie placed the tray on the dresser, though she needn't have bothered. Eating was the last thing on our minds.

******

JULIA arrived in the Dales and made her way along the narrow winding lanes to Longhurst House. She intended to question Millie about the car she'd seen on the forecourt. The one Julia suspected belonged to her brother and Helen.

Parking opposite, she approached the wrought iron gate still barred by the locked chain. She pressed the bell button in the sidewall.

Waiting several minutes for a response, Millie's grandson, Nick, eventually appeared from the house. He'd arrived there only twenty minutes earlier, after being phoned at work by his grandmother to attend. Coming straight from the building site where he'd been labouring, his T-shirt and jeans were coated with cement streaks and dirt.

"Yes?" he asked abruptly, staring at the stranger on the other side of the gate. The alsatians padded out from the house and joined his side.

"I spoke to the woman who lives here a few days ago. Is she about? I'd like to ask her something." Julia thought the man in front of her was a labourer doing some building work on the property.

"What d'ye want to ask her?" Nick fired back.

"I'd rather speak to her," Julia replied.

"I'm Millie's grandson," he said. His shift from an unknown to a connection with the woman, made Julia think it was okay continuing the conversation with him. It was also new information to her that the woman's name was Millie.

"I want to ask her about a car that was parked on the forecourt when I came here the other day," Julia explained. She could see the car was no longer parked there.

"Wait here," said Nick, and walked off across the forecourt towards the back garden. Petra and Rufus remained sitting by the gate, watchful eyes on the stranger standing outside.

Nick stepped on to the chalet porch and knocked on the door. A few moments later Millie opened it, peering out.

"There's a woman at the gate wanting to ask you about the car that was on the forecourt the other day," he told her.

For a second Millie felt rattled. Was it Andrew's sister who'd been here before? Gone away, then remembered seeing his car? She should have hidden it sooner.

"Did you ask her name?"

Nick shook his head.

"Did you ask why was she interested in the car? The one you moved into the garage for me?" Millie continued questioning.

"She didn't say."

"Did you ask?"

"No," Nick stared blankly.

"You wouldn't, would you," Millie replied sourly, knowing the limited intellect of her grandson.

"Tell the woman I'm busy. Say to come back here at six o'clock this evening. I'll see her then."

Nick nodded and left.

Millie returned inside the chalet to continue mixing some chemicals. She felt troubled by the potential intrusion of an outsider who could complicate matters. If it was Andrew's sister, she might have to be quietened.

While Julia waited for Nick to return, she saw a young couple in T-shirts and shorts leaving the front door of the house and approaching the gate. Nearing her, they stopped and smiled.

"Hello," Julia called to them, wondering if they could help. They may have been here when Andrew and Helen had stayed.

The couple continued smiling at her, then turned to walk towards the back garden, disappearing into thin air.

Julia was stunned for a moment, wondering if she'd actually seen them, or if stress was driving her to imagine things. People couldn't just disappear like that. It must have been her imagination. She mustn't let herself fall apart with worry.

As she battled with self-diagnosis of her mental state, Nick returned to tell her Millie would see her at six o'clock that evening. It was a result. At least she wasn't being refused.

"Is there a young couple staying here?" Julia asked him before leaving.

"No," he looked troubled, knowing his grandmother held a young couple in one of the rooms, but sworn to secrecy. Both were unaware they had different couples in mind.

"Why d'ye ask?"

"Doesn't matter," Julia replied, now even more convinced she'd started hallucinating.

She returned to her car and pulled away.

It occurred to Julia that since she'd last been in touch, the local police may have received information about Andrew and Helen's whereabouts, but maybe failed to contact her, even though she'd given them her number to call with any news.

She decided to enquire again, and pulled into a layby.

For several minutes she waited on her phone for an officer to check. He told her no further news had been received. The response brought tears to her eyes, a feeling of hopelessness she might never see her brother or his wife again.

"I think I may have seen their car at a house called Longhurst," Julia persisted in not letting any chance to find them slip away.

"Have you enquired there?" came the question.

"Yes, and I'm meeting the owner there at six this evening."

"Then I suggest you do that first," the officer curtly responded.

Julia realised she wouldn't get any further, and that the officer had possibly concluded she was wasting his time over relatives who might actually be trying to avoid her.

She hung up, now clinging to the hope she would discover more from meeting Millie. Though a hope she felt didn't have any prospect of being realised.

There were several hours to go until six o'clock and Julia decided to drive into Alcott and find somewhere to eat. As she entered the town, her phone started to ring. She pulled over and answered.

"Hello?"

"I'm Detective Sergeant, Alan Parsons."

Julia's heart began beating fast, wondering if the man was calling with good or bad news about Andrew and Helen.

"I understand you're worried about your brother and his wife going missing," the detective continued.

"Yes, have you heard from them?"

"No, I haven't. But I wonder if you could come to the police station in Alcott? I'd like to have a chat."

"What about?"

"We'll talk if you can come here," the detective maintained the mystery.

Julia drove to the station only half-a-mile from where she'd parked, and entered reception approaching the officer at the desk.

"Yes?" the balding, late middle-aged man in uniform raised his head from studying information on the computer screen in front of him.

"Detective Sergeant, Alan Parsons, wants to see me."

A couple of minutes later the dark-suited detective emerged from a side door. Julia guessed he was in his mid-forties, slightly greying short hair and a determined square jaw. He introduced himself and led her to an interview room, completely bare save for a desk and four chairs with a barred high window.

Julia wondered if she'd been called in on suspicion of committing a crime. It was hardly a welcome setting. The detective noticed her concern.

"It's okay," he smiled, his serious face softening. "Just that this room's nearby. Please take a seat," he beckoned her to a chair, then sat down opposite.

He asked Julia to relate her worries about her missing brother and his wife. She told him everything she knew as he took notes in a pocketbook. When she'd finished, he paused for a while, weighing up what he'd heard before saying anything further. For Julia the silence was agonising. Then he began.

"The officer at the desk out front took your call earlier and told me about your concern."

Julia looked surprised. If that was the policeman she'd spoken to, he'd sounded less than sympathetic. Detective Parsons read her face.

"Yeah, miserable sod isn't he," the man smiled. "But he was red hot in his time. Just pissed off being put out to grass these days on desk duty leading up to retirement. Anyway to the point." He sat back in the chair.

"I've been reviewing some missing persons files recently, and the name of that house, Longhurst, has featured several times in reports over the last ten years." He paused.

"I don't know why the connection hasn't been picked up before now. Possibly because other events overtake it, or more likely that records in this area have only recently been entered on a linked computer database. That makes it easier to match connections, rather than being separated into different filing systems."

The detective closed his notebook on the desk before continuing.

"Now I'm thinking it's about time there was further investigation."

The man's words renewed Julia's hope something positive was taking shape that could trace where Andrew and Helen had gone.

"I wonder if you'd like to come along with me and another officer while I interview this..." he re-opened the pocketbook checking a page, "...this Millicent Hendry?"

Julia nodded, needing no second invitation.

CHAPTER 7

AFTER leaving breakfast in our room, it seemed a long time before Millie returned, unlocking the door and smiling triumphantly at us with her constant guard companions behind.

"Time for our visit to the chalet, where everything will be revealed," she said, her expression relishing the fate awaiting us.

For Helen and myself, it sounded like the announcement of a walk to the scaffold.

"Come with me," Millie ordered.

We remained still, continuing to sit on the edge of the bed facing her. She snapped her fingers and the dogs began to growl, warning us not to disobey the command.

I turned to Helen. Her face was growing puce with fury. Although weakened by stress and loss of appetite, I knew from her long built fitness regime she still possessed physical strength.

Helen's eyes almost glowed with hatred for Millie. Any second I could see she was going to spring up and attack. I grabbed her arm, restraining her. Helen could easily demolish the elderly woman, but the dogs would rush in and tear her to pieces. Of course, I'd defend her. I hated the woman just as much. Both of us torn to pieces, however, would hardly be a victory.

Only moments before Millie had appeared again, I'd conceived a last ditch plan of escaping by using the rashers of bacon left untouched on the breakfast plate, and had just put them in my trousers pocket. Millie's return stopped me having the chance to explain the plan to Helen.

My idea was to toss the bacon back into the room as we were leaving, distracting the dogs with food, and slamming the door shut on them. We would overpower, Millie take the door key from her, lock it, then tie her up. That would give us time either to find the keys to the gate chain, or climb over it and escape to raise the alarm.

"Hold tight," I whispered to Helen as we stood up to leave,"we're not through yet."

Entering the landing, I swiftly took the rashers from my pocket, swinging them in front of the dogs for a moment to entice them with scent, then lobbed the bacon into the room.

Their eyes followed the movement for a second as I prepared to leap into action. But the animals remained firmly where they stood. That now familiar, self-satisfied smug smile crossed Millie's face.

"You're not the first to try that trick, except another couple staying here had the idea of distracting the alsatians with food much sooner than you," her voice poured scorn on me. "Their plan failed too."

I felt mortified that my ruse hadn't worked, and at now hearing an admission from the woman we were not the first victims of her imprisonment. But mostly my heart sank at being unable to save Helen from this evil.

We were ushered out of the house and down the garden to the chalet. As we approached, the door opened. Millie's grandson, Nick, stood there.

"He's a good man," said Millie, "just like my dogs, he'll do anything I say."

He moved aside as his grandmother ordered us to enter. The interior looked just like a storage area. A pile of stacked chairs, cardboard boxes, an old sofa and a few disused electrical appliances including a fridge with a missing door. Nothing mysterious inside that Helen and I had conjured in our imaginations.

Desperation makes you cling to the faintest hope. Were we the victims of a sick practical joke? That Millie and her grandson would laugh at us being taken in by a wickedly contrived scam? We could live with that if it meant being free again. The hope quickly began to fade when next she ordered her grandson to unlock another door set back in the room.

"Now make the dogs wait outside," she told him, at the same time waving us to enter the new room. The sight that confronted us was terrifyingly bizarre.

Mounted on a long plinth, side by side stood a row of young couples looking entirely lifelike. Just like exhibits in a waxworks gallery. Except these appeared more vividly lifelike than that, eyes staring as if they held the spark of life.

Our jaws dropped when we recognised some of the figures whose ghostly spirits had manifested in the house, invaded our room of imprisonment, the face in the ceiling, the couples walking through the door, the man in the shower, the unearthly visitation in the darkness delivering a warning that escape was impossible.

"Beautiful aren't they," said Millie, interpreting our horrified amazement at the grotesque line-up as admiration. "They make me feel young again just looking at them. And, as you know, they live in the house with me too. On holiday forever."

She smiled at us again, the insanity in her eyes descending into unfathomable depths.

"They stayed here in past years," she told us proudly. "Their skin is real. Go on, touch the face of that one," she pointed to the figure of a young woman with curls in her dark hair, dressed in a light yellow, short-sleeved top and cream knee-length skirt.

The thought of touching the face was abhorrent, but something urged me to test if the horrific, yet truly skilful display was actually real. My fingers lightly touched the woman's cheek. The face felt cold, but this was no waxwork. It had the texture and softness of human skin.

In reflex, I swiftly pulled my hand away and looked at Helen, each registering our total disbelief that anything so grotesque could really exist. But it did, and now we understood the purpose of our detainment. Millie had plans to add us to her prized collection.

"Of course, to preserve skin in this way," the woman continued oblivious to our terror, "I need a special chemical." She faced us to explain.

"When you arrived I had none because it was a couple of years since my last couple, and the old consignment had deteriorated." She beckoned us to follow her through a side door into another smaller room.

Inside, shelves around the setting contained jars with powder and a variety of different coloured liquids.

"This is the one I was waiting for in the special package delivery I told you about." She pointed to an orange coloured solution in a jar on the shelf. "A very rare chemical only sourced from a plant growing in south east Asia. That's why it took a while for it to arrive."

Millie smiled that devious smile, then took the jar from the shelf and placed it on what looked like a surgeon's operating table. "This chemical is essential in the skin preservation process."

She walked across to a side table on which was laid out a row of metal instruments, much like a surgeon would use to perform an operation.

"I told you when you arrived that I'd learned the skills of taxidermy from my late husband's father when he used to help me with the bed and breakfast business," Millie continued boastfully, starting to put on a pair of surgical gloves.

It flashed into my head that not long after Helen and I came to the house, Millie had started telling us about her father-in-law teaching her a skill. When she reached the point of naming the skill, her dogs had suddenly arrived in the garden barking loudly. It drowned out the word we now realised was taxidermy.

"He was an expert at preserving animals, but after he died I went on to new heights developing techniques for the ultimate lifelike preservation of human beings after their death, as you've just seen," Millie proudly related.

"The messy part is disposing of innards like the heart, liver, brains, you know that sort of thing that makes no difference to outward appearance. They do, however, make a delicious meal for the dogs," she reflected fondly on the treat our insides would provide for her alsatians.

"I'm able to preserve skin, muscles, tendons and bones with chemicals, particularly using the chemical I've now received."

Millie told us of her macabre method unemotionally, as if we were students listening to the consultant surgeon in an operating room. And this was an operating room, we both realised.

The long table was where Millie undertook her taxidermy procedures. And we were her next patients.

I glanced back at the open doorway into the room. Millie's grandson stood there eyeing us keenly.

"Don't be silly," Millie warned, detecting my thought of breaking out. "Nick is very strong. And even if you get past him, my faithful dogs are waiting outside the chalet ready to tear you into pieces. But that would be a wasteful shame."

******

JULIA sat in the back of the police car as Detective Sergeant, Alan Parsons, drove to Millie's house accompanied by uniformed officer, Kirsty Walsh, sitting beside him. He pulled up outside the tall wrought iron gate and they left the vehicle.

Seeing the locked chain around it, the detective pressed the bell button under the name plate Longhurst House.

"I'd like you to identify the woman, Millicent Hendry, when she comes," DS Parsons explained to Julia while they waited for a response. "The woman who told you your brother and his wife had only briefly stayed here."

The man had only just finished his instruction to her when two alsatians came bounding into view from the back garden, racing across the forecourt and starting to bark furiously at the visitors on the other side of the gate.

"I don't think they want us to enter," the detective commented wryly. "Let's wait a little longer to see if someone comes."

They waited a while longer, the dogs growling at them and occasionally jumping at the gate.

"Beautiful animals," said officer Walsh.

"Kirsty has an alsatian," DS Parsons told Julia. "Loves dogs, but I'm not sure she'll have much influence over these."

After several more minutes and repeated attempts to summon someone pressing the bell, the detective could wait no longer.

"Get on the radio and call for assistance to cut the chain and arrange a dog handler," he issued the order to his colleague. "I'm getting a strange feeling about this."

******

"IT'S all quite painless," Millie continued to describe her procedure to us. "I shall quickly put you to sleep, and then keep your bodies in a chill cabinet in readiness for your transformation into lifelike figures. Just like you've seen in the display of my other guests."

She picked up a surgical mask from the side table.

"And your spirits will be able to roam freely around the house and garden at any time day or night." Millie genuinely seemed to think she was doing us a great favour.

I stood there with Helen, both of us stunned into a state of inertia, confronted by the totally bizarre situation unfolding.

"Now ladies first," said Millie, focusing on Helen as if a doctor summoning a patient for a hospital procedure. She indicated a chair beside the table where she stood.

"A little whiff of chloroform and you won't be at all bothered about going into the chiller." Millie put on the surgical mask then opened a bottle on the table, pouring some of the liquid on to a flannel.

"Come on," she beckoned Helen again, nodding towards the chair.

Helen remained still. Inside, my anger was rising to boiling point. The woman was not going to harm my wife.

"It's this, or I let the dogs tear you to pieces, and it would be such a shame to spoil your chances of remaining young and beautiful long after you're dead," Millie threatened icily.

"You evil fucking bitch," I shouted, rushing at the woman to punch the living daylights out of her. Suddenly my body was surrounded by crushing arms, pressing all the breath out of my chest. Nick held me in a bearlike grip.

"Silly boy," Millie called smugly, "you won't escape."

Helen leapt forward giving Millie a hard backhand swipe in the face, sending her sprawling on to the floor, the chloroform flannel flying out of her hand. Helen raced to pick it up, and as Millie, half-stunned, began raising herself from the floor, Helen leapt down straddling the woman, ripping off the mask and forcing the flannel over her nose and mouth.

For a second or two Millie struggled to shake her head free, desperately trying to fend off the attack. Then she slumped back unconscious as the chloroform vapour took effect.

I felt the suffocating pressure on my chest released as Nick cried out in distress seeing his grandmother laying immobile.

"You bastard!" he sprang towards Helen. She rolled off Millie to the side. His frenzy to attack her diverted by terror as he feared his protector might be dead.

"Say something grandma," the man wailed, bending down and flinging the flannel away from her face.

"Get out!" I shouted to Helen as she got up from the floor. In the same moment I rushed forward shunting Nick's arse as hard as I could with my foot as he bent to nurse Millie. He catapulted over his grandmother and went flying face down on the floor.

I knew that wouldn't be enough to put an immensely strong man like him out of action and looked around for a weapon, hoping Helen had found her way to the chalet door. But the dogs!

As I remembered she might be ripped to pieces opening it, Nick had quickly got up and was turning to confront me with manic vengeance bulging in his eyes. I caught sight of a sharp scalpel on Millie's instrument table and grabbed the handle.

Nick was lunging furiously towards me. I backed away holding the blade high in defence, re-entering the room with Millie's horrific display.

I swung round, trying to dodge him, but the giant was almost upon me, arms open wide to grip and crush me. With a furious cry he sprang.

Without even thinking, I swiped the scalpel blade across his face. His oncoming momentum knocked me backwards for a second. Then the searing pain of blood cascading out of the knife slashline made him stop to clutch at the wound. As he drew his hand away and saw it covered red, he staggered back in shock.

A side end of the plinth containing the preserved bodies of young guests Millie had murdered was just behind him. His legs collided with it, making him lose balance and fall backwards on to the nearest figure. In turn it fell on to the next one, causing all of them to crash like a cascading line of dominoes.

I froze for a second, mesmerised as ghostly apparitions began to materialise from the fallen figures. The spirits of the murdered smiled at me for a moment. It was as if their souls had been released from an imprisoned nightmare. A binding spell broken. Then the spirits floated away in different directions, seeming like they were returning to the places from where they had come. In a twinkling they dissolved and were gone.

But Nick was still there, getting up unsteadily from the jumble of the fallen. I didn't plan to stay for another encounter with him.

Running into the outer room, I saw Helen standing by the front door.

"Quick, it's not locked and the dogs aren't out there," she called opening it. I glanced back as we started to leave and saw the bloodied face of Nick advancing at us. We began running across the lawn to head for the main gate and climb over it, when we heard shouting. For a moment it sounded like people were calling our names.

As we approached the screen of overhanging trees across the path to the forecourt, loud barking broke through the shouts. The alsatians were heading our way. We rapidly about turned, racing back to find shelter from them in that hell cursed chalet.

Nearing the open door, Nick appeared blocking the entrance, a self-satisfied smile rising on his blood strewn face. He relished seeing the dogs springing towards us about to attack.

Fury overtook my fear. I launched at him, striking the big man's face with all the power I could summon. The impact didn't so much budge his bulk, as send pain through the raw scalpel wound that had become his weak spot.

Again he tottered back, instinctively clutching the wound. Now off balance, I gave his body an almighty shove to send him tumbling on to the floor.

Helen slammed the door shut just as the dogs reached it. The animals clawed viciously from the outside, barking in fury and preventing any chance of our escape.

Nick was picking himself up from the floor to launch yet another attack, his eyes almost on fire with hatred.

"Try and hold him off for a second," Helen frantically urged, dodging round him and disappearing back to an inner room. Easier said than done as the hulk started rounding on me again.

I darted across the room, nearly crashing into the disused fridge. He was almost on me when Helen reappeared holding the chloroform soaked flannel. She leapt on to his back forcing it over his face. He reached behind trying to grab and dislodge her, but couldn't get a firm hold. In a few more seconds he started to sway, desperately attempting to keep balance. Then the chloroform vapours took over. As he collapsed, Helen leapt off him.

Admiration for my brilliant wife's action coursed through me, but I had no time to praise her. The dogs were still in full fury outside. Once again our way out was barred. Then an idea struck me.

"Let's get Millie and carry her in here," I said. Helen looked puzzled, but trusted me.

We ran back to where she lay unconscious, skirting round the ghoulish sight of deceased bodies, and carried Millie to the outer room.

"Lay her here," I directed, and we placed her on the floor several feet in front of the doorway.

"Now you stand on the other side of the door, and as I open it, let the dogs run in and you run out as fast as you can," I ordered.

"But what about you?" Helen looked alarmed.

"Just do as I say," I shouted, there was no time to waste. I gripped the handle and yanked the door wide open. The raging dogs flew in, then skidded to a halt as they saw their loyal mistress spread on the floor in front of them. They approached her still body, sniffing around her, agitated by something not being right.

"Go!" I yelled at Helen, who still seemed to be hesitating for my safety.

She shot outside, just moments before the alsatians realised they'd been hoodwinked by their quarry. They turned to spring at me with fanged teeth venomously bared for attack.

Instinct took over, literally blacking out memory of me fleeing. All I remember next is yanking the door shut on the outside with all my force and sharp pain in my right arm and leg, with the sound of barking from an enclosure somewhere behind me.

I saw Helen coming to put her arms around me, and what seemed to be a vision of my sister Julia approaching with people in protective clothing beside her. Then memory left me again.

When I came to, I was on a stretcher in an ambulance, deep pain throbbing through the back of my right arm and leg. A female paramedic was rolling up my shirt sleeve.

"Just a little injection," she said. A male paramedic took my arm and inserted the needle.

"This will help."

Blacking out, I woke again wearing a gown on a hospital bed, pain still in my arm and leg, but not so intense with dressings now over the sore areas. Then I became aware of Helen sitting on one side of the bed and Julia on the other.

Helen stood up and bent over to kiss my cheek.

"Welcome back, my hero," she said.

"What happened?" I was mystified.

"The dogs attacked you just before you shut the door on them," she explained. "You were about to escape when they leapt at you from behind, their teeth tearing into your arm and leg. You swung round throwing them off, kicking out, yelling and shouting 'get back, get back'. And they did get back, genuinely surprised for a second by you turning on them. It gave you just enough time to get out and slam the door shut. And it was just in time. They were coming at you so hard, I thought you would be torn to pieces."

Helen kissed me on the cheek again. Her soft lips telling me she was grateful I was still in one piece, if a little shredded.

My apparent heroic fightback was news to me. I had absolutely no recollection of it.

Julia stood up, looking over me.

"Hello brother," she smiled. "You've caused me one hell of a lot of trouble and worry. But then you always did."

******

I was kept in Alcott hospital for another day undergoing check-ups. They also checked over Helen and considered her physically well enough to stay overnight at the local hotel with Julia. Helen's eyes to me, however, still held the trauma of hell we'd been subjected to at Longhurst House.

The mental wounds would take longer to heal. Rest was diagnosed for both of us.

Before we left for home, the detective Alan Parsons, who'd helped Julia, arrived at the local hotel a couple of days later to take statements. I'd been released from hospital and was now also staying there with my wife and sister.

The supernatural angle was not his interest, and we thought he put that down to imaginings arising from stress and imprisonment. Millie's grotesque murders and weird taxidermy was his concern, as well as our kidnapping.

"We've been able to identify names and locations from photos of those poor young couples she killed," he told us. "It's helped us clear up a lot of missing people files from over the years, though I pity their families learning what happened to them."

His words cut through us like a knife. We very nearly became the next couple to join Millie's line-up of horrific trophies and house ghosts.

"What will happen to her?" asked Julia.

"For a psychiatrist and judge to decide," the detective replied. "Most likely she'll be committed to a psychiatric prison."

It came into my mind that Millie was not so much mentally deranged, but possessed by some evil spirit, and that no-one in proximity to her would ever be safe. Powers of the supernatural, however, were beyond my province.

"And her grandson?" asked Helen. "He was under her control."

"Yes, but not totally gone like his grandmother," the detective replied. "He'll probably get a long sentence in a normal prison."

"It's the alsatians I feel sorry for," I said.

"What?" Helen and Julia seemed amazed.

"Well, they were just being loyal to their owner. They had no idea of right or wrong." Though they'd savaged me, I couldn't hold any hate for them.

"The animals have been taken to a dogs' home," said detective Parsons. "Been deemed extremely dangerous, so I don't know what the future holds for yet another couple of Millie's victims."

Helen didn't seem overly convinced with the sympathy. I thought it would be a long time before she could forgive the dogs for severely lacerating my arm and leg, let alone being on the verge of tearing us both to pieces.

Next day Julia drove us home. Our car had been found intact hidden in Millie's garage, but was temporarily impounded while police carried out forensic examinations of the place. It would be transported back to us when they'd finished.

Some weeks later, after Helen and I had rested and felt closer to being restored to our normal selves, Detective Sergeant Parsons rang with the news that several more bodies had been discovered buried in a patch behind the chalet.

"I believe these were the victims of earlier experiments by Millicent Hendry, while she was refining her warped taxidermy skills," he explained.

The evil of the woman, who at our first meeting had seemed so warmly welcoming and friendly, stretched beyond our comprehension. Though admittedly, Helen's sixth sense about Millie did prove correct, as she often reminded me.

"In a back room of the house we found a number of stuffed animals, birds, squirrels and various woodland creatures in display cases," the detective continued. "And in another room we discovered some old books about witchcraft and spells she'd locked in a cabinet. Pages that dealt with capturing the souls of dead people were bookmarked."

It was news to me, but not surprising that Millie was also a skilful practitioner of the dark arts connected to her horrifying human taxidermy, and it accounted for the spirits that wandered her house.

"You told us you'd seen ghosts of the people she murdered for her display?" detective Parsons questioned.

"That's right," I replied.

"It isn't that I disbelieve you," he said. "I can't say if you imagined them or not. Trouble is, they don't make good witnesses in court. But we've got enough material evidence."

As we ended the call, the thought arose that Millie might not be so easily contained behind bars. It sent a shiver through me.

Julia, who'd been a regular visitor to check on how we were coping, came round one evening to have dinner with us. After the meal we relaxed, sitting in the living room with glasses of wine.

"I think you two would do well to take a break away on holiday for a while," she suggested.

Helen sat beside me on the sofa. At my sister's suggestion we both gave each other a knowing look.

Julia suddenly realised she'd gaffed.

"Oh," she smiled apologetically, "but maybe not just yet."

"No, not for a while," I smiled back.

The views of the busy main road at the front of our apartment, and industrial estate at the back, now took on a whole new dimension of secure familiarity, almost broaching on beauty. It brought an old saying to mind. Better the devil you know.

OTHER BOOKS BY THE AUTHOR

I hope you enjoyed *Cursed Souls Guest House*. If you would like to read more of my books they are listed below and available through Amazon. But first a taste of my popular novel:

DEAD SPIRITS FARM

THE PREVIOUS residents of the old farmhouse were lucky. They left just in time. The next couple to own the property were not so fortunate.

Its name, Fairview Farm, disguised a grim title that residents in the nearby village of Calbridge gave to the place. But that was one of the terrifying revelations yet to come in the unfolding story of the new owners.

Benjamin Telford, or Ben as he was known by friends and colleagues, had spent thirty years creating a successful housebuilding company. He was a hands-on man, starting as a building site labourer in his mid-twenties and eventually branching out to form his own construction business.

Now he was more office bound at High Wycombe, a busy town thirty five miles to the north west of London.

Even in his mid-fifties, Ben was still a strong, muscular man, betrayed only in age by greying hair and a furrowed brow. But his thoughts were turning towards taking an early retirement. He'd talked it over with his wife, Eleanor, on several occasions at their home situated not far from the company office.

They'd been married for twenty-five years. Ben had hired the attractive brunette with such beautifully innocent eyes shortly after he'd started his own company. Eleanor's young eyes might have looked innocent, but she was a shrewd accountant and a tempest of authority in her later role as business manager. She'd played a key role in the success of the business.

"There's an old farmhouse going cheap near a small village called Calbridge," said Ben as he sat on the sofa at home looking at properties for sale on his laptop. Eleanor sat beside him reading a book, the sound of the TV quiz show in front of them muted. She stopped reading to look across.

"It's in west Cornwall, not far from the sea," Ben continued, scrolling through the details. "Needs a bit of doing up, but I could make that my project. Might be ideal for our retirement plans."

"Wonder why it's going so cheap?" Eleanor's shrewd mind never lost its inquisitive grip, even though that young, innocent countenance had matured since with a few wrinkles. The rising tide of grey hair, however, was not to be tolerated, held back by the colouring of youthful brunette.

"Looks like someone's done work on the main farmhouse," Ben didn't appear to be taking in his wife's questioning, "but some outbuildings along the side need restoration. Might even be able to offer them as holiday lets. A bit of income." Ben had been office bound for too long. He yearned to use his practical building skills again. He turned to Eleanor.

"It's probably going cheap because of costly redevelopment work needed on the old storage outbuildings." He had been listening to his wife. "If I do it myself then the cost is a lot less."

Eleanor didn't feel entirely settled with the prospect, but it would be good if they could have an early retirement home not far from the sea in a beautiful countryside county where they'd spent holidays in the past, though this area and the village of Calbridge were unfamiliar to them. The couple decided Ben would take a few days off to visit the property and see the local estate agent.

That night Eleanor had an uneasy night's sleep. She dreamed her husband was calling for help from a doorway, his hand outstretched desperately trying to reach her, but being pulled back by some unseen force.

"What's the matter?"

She woke to see Ben sitting up beside her, wondering why she was crying out in distress.

"It's alright," she replied, rubbing her eyes, "just a bad dream."

Eleanor settled to sleep again, only to see her son, Michael, trying to comfort her in the loss of someone dear. Then her daughter Sophie joined him, dressed in sombre dark clothes, attempting to console her. Eleanor jolted waking from the dream, sitting upright on the bed. She stared into the darkness of the bedroom, the subdued glow of a street lamp shining through the curtains giving a little visibility.

"What's the matter ol' girl? What's troubling you?" For the second time Ben sat up beside her, this time placing his arm around her shoulders.

"It's okay. I'm just having some bad dreams," she rubbed her eyes again, as if that would wipe away the fear that had surfaced in her subconscious mind. "Didn't mean to disturb you."

"Probably that cheese and biscuits snack we had before going to bed," said Ben comforting her, "given you indigestion and bad dreams. Settle down my love. Everything's okay."

Her husband's warming words made Eleanor relax. She rested again, thoughts of her son Michael happily married to Australian girl, Lizzie, who he'd met when she'd come to the UK on a month long visit after graduating from university.

Michael was a whiz at accountancy, genetically inherited from his mother, and held the career qualification Lizzie planned to pursue. They clicked. He left his UK job to join her in Sydney, marrying a short time later and setting up their own business.

Eleanor missed him, but felt glad he was happy. Ben had harboured hopes that Michael would join the family business. But that's children for you he'd lamented, also glad his son was building a future.

Daughter Sophie was a single-minded woman, determined not to be drawn into distracting relationships. That is, until she met Leonard.

He was in complete contrast to the type of person everyone thought she would choose for a partner. A mild mannered man, inoffensive, non-argumentative and always happy to embrace another person's point of view. It obviously flummoxed Sophie. She had nothing to contest her fiery personality against. She fell madly in love with him, vowing always to protect him, and they'd been contentedly married for five years.

Sophie had moved from the local area too, now living a long distance away in Scotland, although not so distant as son Michael.

Eleanor drifted into sleep again, but somewhere in the back of her mind Ben's plans for the farmhouse retirement did not rest easily.

******

A COUPLE of days later Ben made the long journey to Calbridge to meet the local estate agent, Justin Turnbull. From the village he was driven to the farmhouse in the agent's car. The salesman was full of enthusiasm for the property.

"Heaps of potential," he described the place, pulling up on the farmstead's paved, red brick frontage.

Ben got out of the car and strode towards the dark oak front door. Justin caught up with him, adjusting his tie knot and smoothing his grey suit.

The original single-storey structure of the greystone farmhouse had been extended in local matching stone by the previous owner, adding first floor accommodation with a pitched slate roof.

Inside, the living room had been enlarged by demolishing the wall to an adjoining old pantry. It was a sizable area with a beamed ceiling. An inglenook fireplace added to the character of the setting.

The kitchen had been extended by taking out the wall of an old scullery. Modern units had been installed, but another part of its earlier look was maintained by a wide fireplace, where a large cooking pot would have once hung over an open fire.

Another room, originally the bedroom, had been converted by the previous owner into a small lounge, retaining the old brick surround fireplace and red tiled floor. Ben instinctively felt there was something odd about the room, but he couldn't place it.

On the first floor the extension provided three bedrooms. Ideal thought Ben for friends and family to stay on visits.

There wasn't much improvement he could make inside the main property, which led him to question, like his wife, why it was on sale well below market value. The outbuildings at the side could be greatly improved, but that wouldn't account entirely for the low price.

"The last owners were wealthy people. Bought the property and did it up after it had been derelict for some years," Justin explained, "then I believe they decided to move abroad. Wanted a quick sale."

To Ben it sounded like an estate agent story, but he was captured by the setting. All around beautiful green meadows with crisp fresh air. Even though late autumn was approaching, the sun blazing in a clear blue sky radiated welcoming warmth through his being.

Beside the farmhouse a wide stony track led to several disused storage outbuildings lining the route, the old walls crumbling and the roofs on them virtually caved in.

The thought returned to Ben they'd be ideal to renovate and offer as holiday lets. Even in retirement he and Eleanor could earn some money from the summer season. The appeal of potential grew in his mind, pushing further away the curiosity of why the farmstead was being sold so cheaply.

Justin smiled inwardly, sensing his client was keen on the property, and glad that Ben's obvious attraction to the setting had distracted him from any close questioning that might lead to the farmhouse's dark history. The sales deal was sealed.

Back home, Eleanor still had misgivings about the purchase, but her husband had made many successful decisions and deals in the past, so she was guided by his plan. And it would be good to share more leisure time together after spending so many years on business, which on reflection had stolen a large chunk of their lives.

A couple of months later the sale completed. Ben gathered his sleeping bag and building equipment which he'd used a number of years back when he worked away from home on projects. The couple had agreed Eleanor would remain looking after the business in the office, while he set off in their Transit van to do some preliminary work preparing the outbuildings for renovation. The first step in the new venture.

But despite this growing positive in life, Eleanor could not rid the sense of dread that kept haunting her. The troubled dreams had continued. She waved goodbye to her husband on the driveway. A terrible omen of it being the last time she would see him alive made her shiver, as if she'd been clasped by a cold embrace from the grave.

Eleanor's fears begin to take form as dark forces descend to strike horror.

Find out what happens next in DEAD SPIRITS FARM by Geoffrey Sleight.

Available on Amazon

MORE BOOKS BY THE AUTHOR

DEADLY ISLAND RETREAT

Trapped on a remote island with ghosts, killers and horrific secrets.

DARK SECRETS COTTAGE

Shocking family secrets unearthed in a haunted cottage.

THE SOUL SCREAMS MURDER

Λ family faces ghost terror in a haunted house.

THE BEATRICE CURSE

Burned at the stake, a witch returns to wreak terror.

THE BEATRICE CURSE 2

Sequel to the Beatrice Curse

A GHOST TO WATCH OVER ME

A ghostly encounter exposes horrific revelations.

A FRACTURE IN DAYBREAK

Family saga of crime, love and dramatic reckoning.

VENGEANCE ALWAYS DELIVERS

When a stranger calls – revenge strikes in a gift of riches.

THE ANARCHY SCROLL

A perilous race to save the world in a dangerous lost land.

All available on Amazon

For more information or if you have any questions
please email me:
geoffsleight@gmail.com

Or visit my Amazon Author page:
viewAuthor.at/GeoffreySleight

Tweet: http://twitter.com/resteasily

Your comments and views are appreciated.

Printed in Great Britain
by Amazon